Vow of the Texas Cowboy

Brides of Bethany Springs
Book Three

Charlotte Dearing

This is a clean, wholesome story of love and family set in late 19th century Texas.

It is the story of Amelia Honeycutt's third and youngest son, Zach, and the woman he falls in love with, in the pine forest of East Texas.

Chapter One
Daisy's Dilemma

Daisy Muldoon

Daisy Muldoon pressed her ear to the floorboard and tapped. A hollow sound greeted her ear, like all the boards before, so she moved to the next board. This time the sound was different. She positioned her head to hear better and tapped again. Her heart leapt. She eagerly started prying the board loose. Maybe, just maybe, she'd finally discovered where her great-uncle had hidden his savings.

Prying a floorboard loose was tricky business. It required a surprising amount of strength, but not too much force. She'd found that out the hard way the first few days after her uncle passed. She'd snapped three boards in half. Three boards she'd need to replace before she and her sisters were forced to vacate the house.

That could happen any day.

The sawmill had been sold to new owners who would expect to find the cottage empty. It was one of the nicer homes, so they'd surely have a tenant move in. Soon, Daisy would lose any claim to her uncle's money.

Easing the crowbar under the edge, she pressed down, gently at first, then with a little more effort. The plank creaked. "Hush, now," she whispered, as if the plank might take note of her request.

The plank protested again, ignoring her command. She closed her eyes. "Please, God. I'm growing desperate. If I don't find Uncle Horace's money, I don't know what I'll do."

The wind rustled across the pine boughs outside the bedroom window.

"Actually, I know what will happen. I'll be stuck in Pineville, which wouldn't be so bad if it didn't mean that Lilly and Poppy would be stuck along with me. Lilly will keep flirting with the lumberjacks and sawmill workers and wind up married and in the family way by eighteen. That's if she's lucky."

Daisy tugged the crowbar again, trying to find just the right amount of force.

"And if I don't find Horace's money, Poppy will be stuck here too. With no schooling. No library. No little friends. And not to paint too grim of a picture..." Daisy's words faded as she pressed down with all her might. The board gave a little. Emboldened, she laughed breathlessly.

"And not to complain about the little things, because this is really not a big thing at all... well, to me, anyway, but for Poppy it's a big thing... if I don't find the money, we won't have a home of our own, and Poppy will never get a puppy."

She wiped her brow, drew a deep breath, and tried to finish loosening the board. Lilly and Poppy were walking up the path, their voices drifting across the wooded yard. Daisy shoved the tool with all her might. A mistake. The board snapped and flew across the room. With a bang, it struck Uncle Horace's staff, a polished length of pine he used when his rheumatism gave him trouble.

Since he'd passed away, Daisy often set the staff by her bedroom door in case any of the loggers tried to give her or her sisters trouble on Saturday nights. It was stout, hard as iron and a trusty weapon. Years ago, as a young woodsman, the *Trusty Mule*, as they called it, had saved Uncle Horace a half-dozen times, or that's what he claimed.

She got to her feet, crossed the room, and set the staff behind the door, out of the way of any airborne floorboards.

Then she hurried back to her task. She peered under the remaining half of the plank. Nothing. It was dark, though. Maybe she needed to let her eyes adjust. Holding her gaze, she willed herself to see the burlap bag where Uncle Horace stashed half his earnings every Saturday payday.

Even after her eyes adjusted, she saw nothing more than an empty hole in the floor.

The front door opened.

"We're home!" Poppy shouted. "Mr. Finch's son gave Lilly a dozen shortbread cookies!"

The girls' footsteps echoed through the house.

"I'm in Horace's room," Daisy called, sitting back on her heels.

Poppy raced down the hallway and came to a breathless stop in the doorway, holding up the paper sack. "We saved you a cookie!"

"One whole cookie?" Daisy frowned with exaggerated annoyance. "One cookie out of a dozen? How generous!"

"I know!" Poppy grinned. "I wanted to eat it, but Lilly wouldn't let me."

Lilly pushed past her little sister to take in the details of Daisy's work. She smirked. "No luck?"

"Not yet but getting closer. That's what I tell myself." Daisy got to her feet and rubbed her shoulder.

"Are you looking for Uncle Horace's gun?" Poppy asked.

Lilly tugged the girl's braid. "He didn't have a gun. He relied on the Trusty Mule."

Poppy's eyes widened. "He did too have a gun. It was small and had a pearl handle and belonged to Grandma. He said when I turned ten, he'd teach me to shoot. He said one day he'd give it to me."

Daisy shook her head. "I wouldn't get your hopes up about any gun. I'm starting to think Uncle Horace didn't have half the things he talked about."

Poppy gasped with indignation. The young girl's face reddened. Her eyes flashed with anger.

Daisy always wondered where her little sister got her temper. Not from her. Not from Lilly or Uncle Horace. Their mother and father were as kind and gentle as could be. Uncle Horace claimed Poppy's temper came from one of the older Muldoons, some troublemaker from the old country.

Horace Muldoon, their great-uncle, was their only surviving relative. He'd sent for them after their ma and pa died of pneumonia. A kindly fellow, he'd cared for them for the better part of a year before he succumbed to his injuries after a logging accident.

With his final words, Uncle Horace urged Daisy to watch over her sisters. She didn't need his direction on that count. There was hardly a time when Daisy *didn't* worry about Lilly and Poppy. Especially since the three girls had come to Pineville, a ragged town filled with itinerant, hard-bitten woodsmen.

"So, what are you looking for?" Poppy opened the cookie bag and peered inside.

Lilly and Daisy shared a smile. Any minute, Poppy would beg for the one remaining cookie.

"Buried treasure," Lilly said lightly.

Poppy jerked her head up. "I thought Daisy said we had loads of money!"

4

Daisy pressed her lips together to silently chide her sister. Lilly lifted a slim shoulder to show the barest hint of an apology. Lilly rarely fretted about anyone aside from Lilly.

"We have plenty of money." Daisy brushed off her hands and picked up the errant plank and covered the hole in the floor, in hopes that no one would twist an ankle on the broken board. Just as soon as she found the missing money, she fully intended to have one of the men in the camp repair the floor. And then the three girls would leave Pineville, never once looking back.

"So why are you tearing up the floor?" Poppy set her free hand on her waist.

"Because our big sister is a pirate." Lilly winked at Daisy. "She likes searching for treasure. That way she can buy you a puppy one day."

Daisy gave a huff of exasperation. Lilly's attempt to distract Poppy was only adding to the problem. Now Poppy would spend the rest of the day talking about the puppy she'd soon have sleeping at the foot of her bed.

Daisy narrowed her eyes to make her displeasure clear.

Lilly snickered. "Maybe *two* puppies!"

Poppy considered this fine bit of news, unaware that she shook the bag holding the last remaining cookie. The cookie knocked around the paper sack. It would soon be nothing more than a heap of crumbs, especially if Poppy kept daydreaming of puppies.

Daisy gave Lilly a disapproving look as she made her way to the kitchen. Without a backwards glance, she felt certain Lilly followed with a self-righteous expression, perhaps even sticking her tongue out at her.

Lilly...

Her seventeen-year-old sister was as lovely as a picture. Everywhere she went, she turned heads. That had been the case even before they'd moved to Pineville. The small lumber town had ten men for every female and the problem of untoward attention had only grown worse.

Daisy unpacked the box of groceries Lilly and Poppy had bought in town. Lilly wandered across the kitchen and gazed out the window. Meanwhile, Poppy studied the remnants of the cookie lying at the bottom of the paper sack.

"This was a lot for you to carry," Daisy murmured as she poured flour into the empty canister on the counter.

Lilly scoffed. "I never carry groceries. Mr. Cook brought me and Poppy in his new buggy."

"He brought us in his new buggy along with the groceries," Poppy added. "Do you want this cookie?"

Daisy sighed. It shouldn't surprise her that a fella from town had squired her sisters home. Mr. Cook was charming. He was elderly and mostly harmless, but even Mr. Cook got a dopey smile on his face whenever he waited on Lilly.

"Do you?" Poppy asked. "Want this cookie?"

"You can have it," Daisy said.

"Mm. Thank you, Daisy!" Poppy sighed. "You're my favoritest sister."

Lilly and Daisy shared a laugh. Poppy liked to bestow the title of "favoritest sister" on either of them whenever needed. She had no qualms swiftly changing allegiance when it served her. Like, for example, where there was the chance to have the last, albeit crumbled, sugar cookie.

"Mr. Cook told me something interesting," Lilly said, returning her attention to a spot outside the window, twirling her hair in that absentminded way.

Daisy glanced past the curtains to see what held her sister's attention. Nothing. As usual. Lilly gathered cotton like no one Daisy knew.

"What's that?" Daisy asked, returning to her task.

"The timber mill sold."

"I know. Some fellow out of Bethany Springs. Mr. A. Honeycutt."

"The A stands for Amelia," Lilly said.

Daisy stopped and turned to her sister. "A *woman* bought the timber mill?"

"No, Daisy," Lilly said in a bored tone. "A man bought the timber mill."

Daisy frowned.

Lilly gave her a solemn look. "A man named Amelia."

"Oh, hush," Daisy said. "I'm merely a little surprised to hear the new owner is a woman."

Poppy nibbled the edge of her cookie. "Is that bad?"

Daisy shrugged. "No. Not really. It's simply my opinion that sawmills are more in line with men's proclivities."

"What's a proclivity?" Poppy asked.

"Why not ask Lilly?" Daisy asked, not able to resist giving her sister a little push-back in return.

"It's a tendency." Lilly gave Daisy a pointed look to prove she was no empty-headed girl.

Daisy waved a dismissive hand.

Lilly explained a little more to Poppy. "Sort of like you have a proclivity for cookies and Daisy has a proclivity for breaking floorboards."

Daisy ignored Lilly's taunting words. "I've always thought of sawmills as men's work. Seems women would prefer more civilized endeavors."

Lilly laughed. "That makes no sense at all. Women are just as eager to make money by whatever means as men."

Daisy ignored the disdain in her sister's tone. Lilly liked to talk about matters as if she knew a great deal of the world. Ridiculous. Especially for a girl who considered books a waste of time and a quick path to ruined eyesight.

"Maybe that's why she hasn't hired a manager yet." Daisy unpacked the basket of eggs. "Because she can't find one to work for her."

"Because she's a *lady*?" Poppy asked with clear astonishment, her half-eaten cookie midair, an inch from her mouth.

"She's *not* going to hire a manager," Lilly replied coolly.

Daisy let out a deep sigh. Lilly always enjoyed dispensing the small bits of news she heard in town. She'd offer it in small bits to keep Daisy guessing.

Mrs. Honeycutt wasn't going to hire a manager. That was both good news and bad news. The three girls could remain in the manager's cottage a while longer. Daisy could continue searching for Uncle Horace's money.

"What is she planning, I wonder." Daisy schooled her tone, hoping to sound unworried. "Run the mill herself?"

Lilly turned to face her as she folded her arms. "She's sending her son, Zachary. He intends to live in this house."

"He can't have *my* room." Poppy shoved the last of the cookie into her mouth.

Lilly twirled a lock of hair around her finger as sparks of amusement danced in her eyes. "He can't have my room either. And I'm sure you won't let him take one step into your room. Guess he'll have to stay in Uncle Horace's room."

Daisy couldn't imagine what Lilly found so amusing. This was a disaster. A first-rate disaster. Her vision swam as she felt more and more wobbly. The Honeycutt family was sending one of the sons to take over the mill...

She had to grip the counter edge to steady herself. Drawing a breath into her lungs, she managed to speak. "When? When is he coming?"

Lilly shook her head. "Not for a few weeks, unless he comes early."

"What will we do?" Poppy asked.

"We'll leave Pineville and go on an adventure." Lilly brushed a lock of hair from Poppy's eyes. "That's what we'll do."

Daisy nodded. She swallowed hard. "Right."

Poppy's eyes sparkled with the prospect of an adventure. "Can we visit the swimming hole before we leave Pineville?"

Daisy groaned inwardly. The last time the girls had donned their swim garments and paddled around the spring, several men from the logging camp spied on them. Or so she suspected. She'd told Lilly that they mustn't return. It wouldn't be prudent.

Lilly always dismissed her concerns, acting as if Daisy worried too much. Daisy hadn't argued. Perhaps she did worry too much, but one of them had to act sensibly. It certainly wouldn't be Lilly.

Despite her misgivings, Daisy found herself agreeing, if only to make Poppy happy.

"Certainly," Daisy said. "Swimming would be delightful."

Poppy eyed her suspiciously. "I'm not leaving Pineville if you don't take me for one last swim. I won't!"

"Of course," Daisy said, trying to sound cheerful.

Lilly's lips curved into a playful smile. She darted out of the kitchen, returning an instant later with Uncle Horace's staff in her hand. "Don't fret, Daisy. No one will dare trouble us. Not if we're armed with the Trusty Mule."

Chapter Two
A Surprising Proposal

Zach Honeycutt

Amelia Honeycutt was as strong and sturdy as any man Zach had ever met. Probably stronger, Zach figured, if character was your yardstick. When Amelia wanted something, you'd be a fool to stand in her way.

Years ago, Amelia had wanted Zach to court Marie McCord, the daughter of Amelia's best friend, Sophie McCord. It never happened. Zach and Marie knew about their mothers' schemes and just laughed about them. They were friends. Very close friends. More like family really... like brother and sister. The notion of courting each other was a grab-your-belly, pick-yourself-off-the-ground sort of joke, to both Zach and Marie.

When school was finished, Zach and Marie saw each other less often. Amelia and Sophie knew they'd probably missed their chance, so they stopped with their not-so-subtle suggestions.

A few years later, Marie married an older man named Grover Patrick, a doctor from Houston who gave up his practice before he turned fifty. He said it was to raise a family, but folks wondered if his shaky hands and unsteady gait hadn't been the real reason.

Zach didn't know much about Grover at the time, but what he did know he wished he didn't. As a member of the Bethany Brotherhood, Zach knew about the unsavory elements in

Bethany Springs. He knew that the town barber ran a secret gambling club, a harmless pastime for most of the fellows, but not for Marie's new husband. Grover tended to drink more than he should, a fair amount more, unfortunately, and he often had a hard time getting home after a late night of gambling.

Several months ago, Grover had visited the club, overindulged, then fallen into the river. When he didn't return to the McCord Ranch that night, the Bethany Brotherhood banded together to search for him. They found him a few days later, drowned.

It was a sad time, with Marie still so young and already a widow. A small ceremony was held on the McCord Ranch and Grover was laid to rest in the family plot.

Now, three months later, the McCords hosted a small gathering of friends in their home, in hopes of cheering up the grieving widow. Dressed in black, Marie greeted the guests with her usual elegant poise. She didn't seem terribly distraught. If anything, Marie acted happy to see friends and family. She spoke of great plans and an exciting future for herself and her young daughter, Madeline.

Zach poured two cups of punch, crossed the parlor, and offered her a cup. She sighed wearily.

"Are you tired?" he asked.

"Yes. Tired of grieving." She took a dainty sip.

Zach wondered how much she knew of her husband's vices but wisely held his tongue. "You're looking very well."

"That's because I've decided I'm done with grieving."

Zack took a swallow of the too-sweet punch, wondering where this might be going.

12

"Grover was a good man, in some respects, but in other ways he had his own notions of what it meant to be a good husband and father. In a way, I've been grieving a long time."

Zach's heart ached for his childhood friend. He hated to see her suffer. Hated to think she'd been unhappy. "Marie, I'm sorry."

She shrugged a shoulder. "I've never said those words aloud. I suspect my mother knows, but still. It's not something I could say to her. It would upset my father too."

He wished he could soothe her with some well-chosen words. He couldn't find the right words, though, so he remained silent.

Marie tilted her head toward the other side of the room where Sophie and Amelia stood, eyeing them with distinct interest. The look in Mama's eye should have sent a jolt of fear down Zach's spine, but he was racking his mind for some word of comfort for Marie.

"Would you believe my mother and yours are scheming again?" Marie whispered.

"About what?"

"They think they'll finally get their wish," Marie said softly as her eyes flickered with irritation.

"Wish? Scheming?" A knot of fear wrapped around his insides. He glanced at the fruit punch. Something in the drink wasn't agreeing with him. He set his cup aside. He gave his mother and Sophie a furtive look, noting they still stared. He straightened his tie. It was already straight. He ran his tongue over his teeth but didn't detect any spinach from the fancy dip Sophie always served. Why were they staring?

"I think they suspect," Marie said. "Grover wasn't much of a son-in-law. I've spent most of the last year living with my

13

mother and father. I'm sorry my daughter has lost her father, but beyond that-"

"Stop it, Marie." Zach shook his head. "Stop right now."

"My mother wants me to remarry as soon as possible. She wants me to marry you, Zach. Your mother wants that too."

Zach began coughing. It started as a slight tickle at the back of his throat. If Marie had said something, anything really, he might have been able to stop the hacking cough. She simply held her gaze as he gasped for breath.

Slowly, his coughing abated. Marie picked up his cup and offered him what punch remained. "Here you go. *Darling.*"

He grimaced as he took the delicate cup. With a quick motion, he drained the contents and handed the cup back to her. "You know I'd do anything for you, Marie. You're the sister I never had. Which pretty much sums up the whole problem."

Marie plucked a piece of lint from his collar. She lifted her gaze, her wan smile curving into a slight curl of her lip. "Zach, you're the last man in the world I'd marry. In fact, I'm never marrying again."

Zach let out a sigh which turned into a relieved chuckle. "You sort of scared me for a minute."

She kept her expression fixed, a hint of a feminine snarl on her lips. "Oh, you're not off the hook, Zach Honeycutt. I need your help."

"With what, exactly?"

Marie gave a throaty chuckle, the same exact laugh she gave as a girl, just before beating him at checkers or marbles. With three older, incorrigible brothers, Marie had learned how to play pranks early on. She knew just how to take care of herself. The only female more cunning and calculating than Marie was his mama.

"I understand you're heading off to East Texas, is that right?" she asked, her tone innocent.

"East Texas?" he asked cautiously. Zach felt afraid. It had been years since Marie had scared him. Years. But she was doing a fine job right there in the middle of the McCord's parlor.

"Yes, or no?" she demanded.

"Y-yes. I am."

"For how long?"

"Not sure. A few months. Maybe longer. Maybe a year. My mother bought a mill and wants me to run it until she can sell it. Not sure how long I'll be there."

Marie smiled triumphantly. "Perfect."

Zach held his breath. Somehow, he felt sure that Marie's idea of perfect wouldn't be the same as his version of perfect.

"I accept your proposal," she said sweetly.

"Proposal?" he choked.

"It's just a year."

"A year..."

Marie continued. "It will give me plenty of time to take a trip to visit a childhood friend. A trip to England."

"England?" Zach demanded. "*England?*"

"Quit shouting. Yes. England. Perhaps even France."

"Marie, surely now is not the time for you to go on a trip. Right after you lost your husband?"

She gave an inelegant snort. "This is the perfect time to take a little trip. I've just learned how much Grover left me, which is a considerable sum of money, especially since he always kept me on a severe budget. He wouldn't even consider a simple trip to the Texas shore, much less abroad."

"What about the baby?"

"I intend to take Madeline with me. I'll hire a nurse to help. The three of us will leave Galveston and sail to Southampton so I can visit my dearest friend, Harriet, a girl I've known forever. I'll have a chance to show off my daughter and meet her children."

Zach scrubbed a hand down his face. He sure didn't want to marry Marie, but he still felt a strong protective feeling for her.

Marie looked petulant. "I've never seen Harriet's children, thanks to Grover's tightfistedness."

"Can't Harriet just send you a picture?"

"Spoken like an ornery male. No, she can't send a picture. I want to *see* the children. I want to sit with Harriet, drink tea and eat scones, talk, reminisce, see the sights. Her husband is very well-to-do and has promised to show the two of us a fine time. Opera, fine dinners, theater."

None of that sounded like a fine time to Zach but he figured he'd best keep his opinions to himself.

"I want to have fun!" Marie said softly. "My father would never let me travel as a single woman, but he will let me go if I'm engaged to be married."

Dread settled over his heart. "My word, I see where this is going."

"All my life, I've answered to my parents or to an indifferent husband. I'm exhausted by the grieving and all the endless expressions of sympathy. I want to escape Texas and live for a while without answering to anyone."

She looked at him with tear-filled eyes, but he refused to give in to her theatrics.

"I don't know about any of this."

"I'm not asking for your approval."

Zach was stunned and had a hard time schooling his features, there in the quiet of the McCord parlor.

"I have a say in whether or not I get engaged," he muttered.

"Of course, you do, my *darling*. We won't be *actually*-engaged, we'll be *pretend*-engaged. And I can go one step further. I will be the one to be pretend engaged. You don't really have to do anything. You'll be hundreds of miles away, where no one knows a thing about you. You can just live your life, and all the sweet people of Bethany Springs, especially those two over there," she said, nodding toward Sophie and Amelia, "will look forward to the day next year when we end our engagement in holy matrimony."

"But that's not how this will end, Marie. We're not getting married."

"Sweetheart, we can end the engagement when I get back from my travels. I promise, I will make it easy on you. I'll tell everyone my heart remained in France with a young man I met on my journey, and I simply cannot proceed with a marriage to a man who I love less."

"This is the craziest idea I've ever heard."

"It's not crazy." She gave him a pointed look. "More punch? My sweet?"

He grumbled and shook his head. It galled him to think she'd drawn him into her plan. And yet, his mother was constantly hounding him to find a nice girl and settle down. If he played along, maybe his Mama would leave him be. That part sounded pretty good. The rest, not so much.

Marie turned away, her silken skirts rustling, leaving him to stew. She walked across the room with her usual graceful manner and genteel smile. Holding out a slender hand, she greeted an arriving guest and thanked them for coming in her time of need. Yes, it was sad, she murmured, turning to glance over her shoulder, giving him a sly smile.

Marie couldn't be serious about any of it. That's what he told himself. She was just talking nonsense and would set aside her absurd plans. He was sure.

Chapter Three
A Hasty Prayer before the Storm

Daisy

A steady rain fell through the night, but the morning dawned bright and sunny. Daisy noted a wave of gratitude for the good weather as she rose from her bed. A clear day was good for business, which Daisy had come to fully appreciate. With two sisters depending on her, and bills to pay, it was important to make money whenever she could.

She brewed a pot of coffee and proceeded to make sandwiches for the hungry loggers, customers who paid a good price for her savory lunches. She sliced the loaves of bread she'd made the night before. Next, she cut the ham she bought from the butcher along with the block of cheddar.

Finally, she spread the bread with mustard and set a generous slice of ham and sharp cheddar on top of every other slice of bread. When she finished, she wrapped each sandwich in a swath of wax paper and tucked the small parcel into her basket.

Serving lunch to the loggers had saved her family from poverty. The venture was nothing more than an act of desperation.

After Horace succumbed to his injuries, Daisy had no money. No prospects. The idea came to her in the wee hours of the morning, the day after they'd said their goodbyes and laid their kindly uncle to rest.

The inspiration turned out to be a Godsend.

It was a small enterprise to be sure, but it was reliable. The lumberjacks were always hungry and happy to buy her wares.

Several mornings a week, she rose at dawn to make sandwiches. Late morning she'd walk to the camp, pulling a wagon with the boxed lunches. Near the loggers' shanties, she left the road and took the path into the forest, making her way through the towering pines. The walk gave Daisy a chance to admire the beauty of the forest.

She made a point to arrive as the foreman blew the whistle for lunch. The men would wander to the small clearing, looking for her and smiling when they saw her standing by her wares. Usually, she was the only person selling sandwiches which resulted in her selling everything in less than ten minutes.

Most of the men were courteous, but a few of the men would routinely ask about Lilly, always with that same troubling gleam in their eye. Daisy didn't mind the questions so much. She knew perfectly well Lilly was the pretty one, and she herself was the plain one. What bothered Daisy was the way the men leered or elbowed each other at the mention of Lilly's name.

Daisy might tease her sister every chance she got, but she couldn't tolerate strangers making comments about Lilly.

"Are you and Lilly true sisters?" one of the workers asked as he paid for his lunch.

"What do you mean?" Daisy tried to keep a light tone as she took his payment and dropped the coins in her pocket. "True sisters?"

The men stood around her wagon, others sat nearby, sprawled across chairs and tables under the pine trees. All of them seemed to find the question amusing.

"What he means is, do you two girls have the same father and mother?" one of the men called from where he sat on the edge of the picnic area.

"Yes. We do." Daisy spoke cautiously. She prayed the men wouldn't say something coarse about her younger sister. That had never happened, but she suspected they talked plenty the minute she left.

"We do have the same father and mother," Daisy said, trying to keep her dignity. "Why do you ask?"

She cringed. The question had practically jumped from her lips, inviting more awkwardness. Thank heavens she'd left Poppy at home.

The man who'd asked the question had retreated a few paces and leaned against a stout pine trunk, his wax-paper wrapped sandwich in one hand and his hat in the other. He blushed, sensing her discomfort. Daisy felt a little sorry for him. Clearly, he was one of the more polite workers.

"Go on, Cody," shouted one of the men. "We want to hear why you're asking."

The men spoke amongst themselves, a few of them leaning their heads close and chuckling over some shared joke.

The young man, Cody, looked aggrieved. "You all shut up. I'm only asking because Miss Daisy has yellow hair, and her two sisters have hair the color of a copper penny."

Daisy made light of the matter. "My mother had red hair. I always wished I had gotten her pretty red ringlets like my sisters."

"Your hair is mighty pretty too, Miss Daisy," Cody said. "The color of a fresh egg yolk."

The men hooted with laughter. The young man reddened and frowned at his companions which only made them laugh all the more. Daisy had to smile too, despite her

21

embarrassment. No one had ever compared her hair to egg yolks.

All her life, Daisy had admired her sisters' lovely hair. Poppy and Lilly had glorious manes of auburn hair, spun into a soft profusion of curls. Both girls required an extra half-hour each morning to tame their curls into a civilized arrangement. Lilly preferred to manage her own hair while Poppy often grew impatient and demanded Daisy's help.

"I confess that I envy my sisters." Daisy patted her ordinary blonde locks. "I ended up with my father's blond hair. No curls, just plain yellow hair. Nothing special. Blonde hair that's straight as a pin."

The young man chuckled. "Well, I think you're as pretty as can be."

Daisy waved off his flattery as she gathered the linen cloth she'd draped across the table. The men all cheered Cody's attempts at flattery. They poked fun at the poor fellow, accusing him of trying to get extra fixings on his sandwich.

It was times like this that Daisy felt warmly toward the loggers. They were rough around the edges, to be sure, but they couldn't help their lack of manners. They hadn't spent much time in the company of women. Daisy was certain, these men did not realize how their bawdy humor made her uncomfortable, and if they did, she was certain they would stop. That's what she told herself.

Daisy did not want to instruct or correct the men. It wasn't her place to judge. They could remain just as they are. She just wanted to leave, as soon as possible. She yearned for a life far from the logging camp, for her sake, but especially for that of her sisters. Still, she liked to think that the meager lunches she served the loggers made their difficult lives a little easier.

"I'll see you gentlemen in a few days," she announced.

"In a few days. When?" one of them asked.

"Friday."

They all shouted their stern disapproval. "Friday? That's too long! Why aren't you coming tomorrow or the next day?"

Daisy refused to explain her reasons. For one, she needed to spend more time searching for Uncle Horace's secret hiding place where he'd hidden his money. That was the most important matter. If she couldn't find his money, she and her sisters would be thrown into desperate circumstances, especially when the Honeycutt fellow arrived. He'd expect an empty, clean house, one that didn't have three girls and twenty broken floorboards.

The other reason Friday would be the next visit was her promise to take Poppy swimming. Ever since Daisy had spoken of leaving Pineville, Poppy had fretted endlessly, especially since Daisy didn't know where they'd go afterwards. Daisy wanted a day for Poppy to have fun and forget her fretting.

When she returned home, she found Lilly napping in her room. Daisy couldn't help a slow simmer of resentment. The porch hadn't been swept. The breakfast dishes sat in the washbasin, soaking in the cold water. The laundry flapped on the line while storm clouds gathered on the horizon.

Poppy sat at Uncle Horace's desk, rummaging through the bottom drawer. For an instant, Daisy entertained the wild hope that her sister had found the money. It made no sense. Poppy hadn't been searching. She hardly cared about the missing burlap sack. What was more, Daisy had already searched the desk a dozen times.

"Hello there, my sweet Poppy." Daisy leaned into the room. "What are you doing?"

"I'm looking for great-uncle's gun. He said it was fancy. When I find it, I'm going to sell it to Mr. Cook at the mercantile."

Daisy didn't bother explaining for the tenth time that there likely wasn't a fancy gun anywhere in the cottage. She was far too weary to start a debate with Poppy. Her little red-haired sister was as tempestuous as most redheads.

"Did you do your lessons?"

Poppy shook her head. "I'll do them soon."

She went back to exploring the desk, humming as she worked, shuffling papers around as she searched the depths of each drawer. Daisy sighed and went to her room to add her earnings to the coffee can. She shook the can, rattling the coins absentmindedly.

When she and her sisters came to Pineville, her uncle had promised the three girls would never want for anything. As a supervisor of a large logging team, he earned a good wage. He doted on the three sisters, especially Daisy. He didn't want her to work in the camp, claiming it wasn't fitting for a gently raised young lady.

Uncle Horace hadn't ever married and relished the notion of having three nieces to watch over. He'd come home each evening, tired but pleased to see his "girls." After dinner, he'd light his pipe and tell them stories of his travels across America.

They'd enjoyed a happy sense of family right up until he'd been injured in a logging accident.

Once again, the three girls were alone and adrift.

Daisy pushed the sad memories aside and tucked the coffee can beside a stack of books.

Lilly appeared in the doorway, looking rumpled and sleepy from her nap. She came to Daisy's side and silently wrapped an arm around her shoulders. With her other hand, she lifted the coffee can and shook the coins.

"Sounds promising," she murmured.

"The men were asking for you, talking about your pretty hair, how it's so different than mine."

Lilly sighed. "I'd give anything for your pretty, straight hair. I've heard of girls straightening their hair by washing and wrapping it around cans while it dried. Can you imagine?"

Daisy tugged one of Lilly's stray tendrils. "No, I can't imagine. Who would want to give up such glorious curls?"

Lilly gave an inelegant snort. "And who would want to wrap their hair around cans? Can you imagine how heavy they would be? The weight pulling on your hair."

"Heavy?"

"Yes. Heavy. That's why I haven't tried it."

"Heavy... you mean the cans?"

"Of course, I mean the cans. How could a girl stand that sort of weight on her head?"

Daisy stared at her sister. Sometimes Lilly said the daftest things and made Daisy wonder about her sister's mind. Surely, she wasn't that empty-headed. Surely.

Lilly looked affronted. "What?"

Daisy winced, hoping she hadn't shown her disbelief. It wouldn't do to look like she thought Lilly was a ninny. Lilly always noticed.

Daisy cleared her throat. "I have to assume the idea is to use *empty* cans. Not full cans."

As Lilly's cheeks reddened, Daisy almost felt sorry for her. She ought to restrain herself. After all, she was the older sister. But she couldn't hold back a small chuckle.

"Lilly, you are a little simple-minded at times," Daisy said, trying not to give in to a burst of amusement. "But it's quite endearing. Really."

"No more simple-minded than you are." Lilly said, sulking.

Daisy tugged her sister close and took a moment to embrace her. "I do love you. Very much."

"Oh hush," Lilly grumbled.

After a long moment, Daisy loosened her hold. There was so much to do, especially with the coming storm. The room had grown dark. A rumble of thunder reminded Daisy of the laundry on the line. She left Lilly's side, hurried outside carrying her basket, and began the task of gathering the clothes.

A raindrop splashed on her hand. Another followed, hitting the top of her head. The trees swayed with the force of the coming storm, whistling through the pine needles.

The back door of the cottage slammed shut. Poppy skipped across the yard, laughing at the stray raindrops that fell here and there. She twirled, arms outstretched, with her face raised to the sky.

The sun appeared for an instant from behind a steel-gray cloud. Beams of sunlight cast dappled shadows across the grass.

Daisy stared at the fantastic scene, brilliant sunshine from the west surrounding her young sister, tall, dark thunderclouds towering to the north. *God is in everything that matters.* Her uncle said that a hundred times, and at that moment she knew God was all around her.

Poppy continued to spin, giggling, and singing the words to a song. Her soft curls bounced and danced in the wind.

Instantly the sun vanished again. The wind gusted. The billowing clouds were nearly over them now. The temperature dropped with the wind, bringing the sharp scent of rain.

Daisy resumed her task, working as quickly as she could to gather the clothes.

"Watch over your sisters," her great-uncle had implored. She'd agreed at once. Of course, she had.

If only she'd thought to ask about the money he'd hidden. He'd always shielded her from such matters. He wanted her to rest assured he'd take care of them. She hadn't dared ask about his money, for the question seemed rude and blunt. Worse, she would have been admitting that he was dying. How could she mention the painful subject? How could she suggest her dear uncle was not long for the world?

Poppy became so dizzy she toppled to a heap in the grass. Her giggles drifted on the swirling breeze. A rumble of thunder rolled across the sky, followed by a gust of wind that made the laundry toss and snap.

Daisy ought to hurry and finish, but she had a thought. God was right here, right now.

She closed her eyes. "Dear Lord, please help me. Help me care for my sisters," she whispered. "Show me the way."

Chapter Four
An Early Departure

Zach

Zach would always have a soft spot in his heart for Marie. He knew it. They were family.

And Zach would do nearly anything for Marie. Nearly anything. But this. This was too much. He could hardly stay quiet amidst her shenanigans. It had been two days since the gathering in the McCord home. Two days since all heck had broken loose.

Mama and Sophie laughed and cried about dreams coming true, and wouldn't poor Grover be pleased how things turned out.

Meanwhile, Marie was clearly ready to leave. She'd already announced her travel plans to see Harriet. She told her mother it would give her a chance to shop for a wedding dress. When Sophie pitched a fit, refusing to let her leave, Marie played the part of grieving widow who needed a trip abroad. She explained that she'd hired a nurse for her young daughter and arranged travel on a ship leaving Galveston in the next few days.

Zach had only wanted to get on with his work in Pineville. He yearned to take up the reins of the sawmill so he could set things right and hopefully return home sooner rather than later. He prepared for his trip, or tried to, but quickly found himself in hot water with his mother.

Now, instead of being the dutiful son taking on a troubled sawmill, Amelia blamed him for Marie's ambitious travel plans. Things came to a head the morning he intended to leave Bethany Springs.

"Seems to me you two could have traveled together," Mama snapped over breakfast. "Instead, Marie's talking about a grand tour. A grand tour! That's the sort of thing rich, spoiled young women do, not a respectable widow who also happens to be the mother of a young child."

The breakfast was supposed to be a sort of sendoff. A farewell meal with his two brothers and dear mother. Instead, he found himself mired in the details of a mock engagement, all thanks to Marie's scheme.

Zach could hardly argue, not without giving away Marie's plans. He gritted his teeth and waited for his blood to stop steaming. It didn't help that Simon and Daniel sat across from him, trying their best not to smirk. Just that morning Daniel questioned Zach's judgment about getting married so soon after Grover's passing.

Simon, the middle brother, didn't bother with questions or proper manners. Instead, he flat-out called Zach a mama's boy, a fella who would do anything to win favored status among the Honeycutt boys. While Zach seethed, Simon touched his nose and grinned.

Zach clenched his fist in warning.

"Sophie spent yesterday in my parlor, crying her eyes out." Amelia shook her head. "Robert's barely speaking at all, which is always a bad sign. Marie tried to explain she's going to London to get fitted for a wedding dress, but we have wedding dresses right here in Texas."

Pain jabbed the spot behind Zach's eye. A wedding dress? For a woman who vowed never to marry again.

"I'll see if I can talk some sense into her," Zach muttered. "I'm not leaving for Pineville for a bit."

Simon nodded. He knit his brow, a poor attempt to look thoughtful. "Maybe Daniel and I can give you a little advice, seeing as we're both family men. What do you say, Daniel?"

"I wish you would," Amelia groused. "Clearly, Zach needs a few pointers."

Simon agreed. "Anytime I get into a bad way with Virginia, I invite her on a picnic."

Zach clenched his jaw.

"Well, that's mighty nice," Daniel exclaimed.

"I even pack the basket myself," Simon boasted. "I have to say it works out better that way seeing as Goose isn't the best cook, though you never heard that from me."

Amelia smiled fondly at Simon before turning her gaze to Daniel. "What about you? What do you do when you've caused Molly some small offense?"

Daniel looked affronted. He seemed to consider the question, mulling it over silently.

Simon grinned. "Mr. Perfect? Daniel never offends anyone. He's the one making us all look bad."

Amelia chuckled before she remembered she was mad at Zach. Her smile faded. Her eyes darkened. "Your fiancée is talking about traveling for months. Months! I'm not sure who Sophie will miss more, her daughter or her granddaughter. You have to speak to Marie before you leave Bethany Springs."

Simon took a biscuit from the breadbasket. "Want me to pack you a picnic, Romeo?"

Daniel laughed. "Romeo. Ha. I never knew Zach cared for Marie." He sobered, gestured wordlessly a time or two before continuing. "Of course, we all care for Marie. She's a lovely girl. We'd do anything for her."

Simon shook his head. "We'd do *almost* anything for her. Zach's taken that sentiment a little further, I'd say."

Zach considered how many ways he'd like to cause Simon a little grief. Anything to wipe his brother's gloating smirk from his face. It was clear that Simon wasn't buying any of the engagement story, but that wasn't stopping him from having a little fun.

Daniel seemed to have bought the entire tall tale. Of course, he had. Daniel was kind, noble and generous to a fault. He was also a tad gullible. Then again, Zach had to consider if *he* was the gullible one. After all, he'd gotten himself hoodwinked into a lengthy engagement, one he never wanted.

"Marie is mighty pretty," Daniel said, trying to bolster Zach's position.

"She is indeed," Simon said, winking at Zach. "Is that what won you over, Zach? Her beauty? Or was it something else? Maybe it's the way she likes to split hairs. Remember how we used to say she'd argue with a haystack?"

"Maybe that's it," Zach agreed. If he tried to argue with Simon, it would only prolong the ordeal. Marie wasn't the only person who'd argue with a stack of hay.

"Or was it how demanding she is?" Simon continued. "Remember the time Robert hired a fancy cook all the way from New Orleans for Marie's sixteenth birthday party? The fella had been trained in some fancy school. Robert spent a fortune. Was Marie satisfied? Nope. She had a tantrum because the cake was raspberry instead of strawberry."

Amelia shook her head. "It was the other way around. Marie wanted strawberry and Pierre Whatsit made raspberry."

"Oh, I do recall that night." Daniel said giving Zach a sympathetic look. "Marie was a little... miffed."

Zach, Simon and Amelia all turned to Daniel, as if he'd just said something in another language.

"You know, miffed. Like, mad about her dessert not being what she expected."

Daniel rarely spoke poorly of a person. Even describing Marie's response with a word like "miffed" was saying something for Daniel Honeycutt.

Zach, meanwhile, drummed his fingers on the table, wondering what he'd done to deserve any of this. Nothing. Not one danged thing. He should have left for Pineville a few weeks ago. If only he'd known.

Simon took a break from his storytelling which provided Amelia with a chance to share her own recollections. "Do you boys remember when Marie went through her cream puff stage? Poor Sophie had to bake cream puffs fresh for every meal, otherwise darling Marie refused to eat. She turned her nose up at everything aside from cake. We all started calling the girl Marie Antoinette!"

Daniel and Simon joined their mother in a hearty round of laughter. Zach sat quietly, wondering if he could just slip out of Bethany Springs without anyone noticing. As the laughter subsided, Amelia wiped tears from her cheeks.

"Don't any of you tell Sophie I said that bit about Marie Antoinette." Amelia waved her index finger at the three of them. "Sophie would never forgive me."

Zach had darned near summoned the needed courage to ride over to the McCord Ranch to talk to Marie face to face. Just when he was about to take his leave, a McCord ranch hand came to the door with a note from Marie. Mama brought it to the dining room and handed it to Zach. The room grew silent. He opened the envelope, his heart thudding with dread. For the life of him, he couldn't imagine any note from Marie that might hold good news.

He read the words once and then once more for good measure. Letting out a weary sigh, he lifted his gaze and smiled. "She's left Bethany Springs. She managed to get passage on an earlier ship and has taken Maddy and the nurse."

"Where exactly is she off to?" Mama asked.

"I'm not sure." Zach eyed the note. "Probably England to see her friend Harriet, if I'm remembering correctly."

Amelia took a swallow of her coffee, eyeing him over the rim. She set the cup down and folded her hands in front of her. "I must say, son. You're taking this rather well."

Simon nodded. "You *are* taking this well. So well. If I didn't know better, I'd almost believe you're happy she's set off on her travels."

Daniel grumbled. "That's uncalled for, Simon. Let up, would you? Zach doing his darned best to deal with this heartache."

Simon chuckled and wiped an imaginary tear from his eyes.

Zach ignored Simon as he noted a deep gratitude for Daniel's kind sensibilities. The eldest Honeycutt boy had certainly gotten more than his fair share of noble traits.

Simon, to his credit, refrained from laughing outright at Daniel's words. Nor did he torment Zach with any other teasing comments. Instead, Simon kept his lips buttoned or mostly buttoned. He managed to eat three more biscuits loaded with butter and honey, a teasing smile playing on his lips.

Mama said little apart from a few words of sympathy for Sophie and Robert. The McCords would miss Marie and little Madeline something fierce, she was certain.

"Guess there's no time for a tearful goodbye," Simon said.

"Guess not," Zach shot back.

Simon chuckled.

Zach held the note and felt the weight of the world slip from his shoulders. Marie's departure seemed like a reprieve. He excused himself from the table, giving a quick comment about getting on his way to Pineville and set out for the barn to prepare for his travels.

It would take him a few days to reach the other side of Texas. Despite the long ride, he didn't need much in the way of provisions. It took him less than an hour to load his things onto a pack mule. He saddled his best horse and went to the house to say goodbye.

His mother and two brothers waited on the porch. All three came down the steps to wish him well.

Mama held him a long while. "You take good care. Sawmills are perilous endeavors. I'll sell the whole operation if you ask me to."

"I'll write with news." He kissed her on the forehead.

"I plan to head that way in a few weeks to look in on my youngest boy," she said, her voice choked with tears. "Gosh, I'm getting sentimental in my old age."

"That would be swell." He smiled, emotion washing over him as he rested his palms on her shoulders. Just a few hours before, he'd been in trouble with his mother, but she'd gotten past her annoyance. Probably because he was leaving. Mama never liked her sons venturing too far from home.

"I look forward to seeing you, Mama." He nodded toward Simon and Daniel. "Just don't bring my pesky brothers."

She smiled through her tears. "I make no promises."

Simon and Daniel laughed and grumbled good-naturedly. They both embraced Zach and wished him well. Neither said a word about Marie, thankfully. Zach swung into his saddle, tipped his hat, and bid his family a final word of farewell. With that, he set off for the East Texas town of Pineville.

Chapter Five
Fun at the Swimming Hole

Daisy

After weeks of searching Horace's room for the money, Daisy had little to show for her work. Almost nothing, unless she counted the loosened, broken floorboards, or the gaping holes scattered across the room.

Her sisters came to the door often to check her progress. Lilly regarded the holes and broken planks with a wry grin. She probably figured that she'd marry one of the wealthier loggers and thereby help the family. Daisy couldn't think of anything worse.

Poppy acted as if the whole matter was a game, specifically a game of hopscotch. She jumped over the holes, counting her steps as she made her way from one side of the room to the next. The youngest Muldoon didn't worry too often, thankfully, and likely assumed things would work out one way or another.

In her nineteen years, Daisy had learned that things don't always work out. Sometimes things turn bad and there's nothing you can do to make it better. She'd also seen that, sometimes, her own efforts could make a difference in how things turned out. Prayers to God. Hard Work. This is all she could do or think about since Horace's passing.

It was time for a day off.

She woke early in the morning just as dawn lit the horizon. "I'm not searching for the money today," she whispered to reassure herself. "I'm spending the day with my sisters. Swimming. The whole day. It's settled."

Daisy had been so focused on household duties that she hadn't considered matters of the heart. In the past, she'd been sure to pray with her sisters and spend time together, merely enjoying each other's company. She yearned to give both girls some happy memories from their time in Pineville. Not just recollections of the sad times.

She knelt beside her bed to say her morning prayers. After she was done, she dressed in a light, muslin dress and began to make a lunch for the three of them to enjoy at the spring. Poppy and Lilly rose, wandering into the kitchen like a pair of sleepy owls.

Once Daisy told them about her plans, they sprang to life and helped pack the picnic basket. They chattered excitedly and soon the three girls were on their way to the springs. Lilly and Daisy carried the basket together. Poppy begged to carry Horace's staff.

"I promise to take excellent care of the Trusty Mule." To prove her point, she swung it over her head, accidentally knocking a dead limb loose. The brittle branch fell with a crack, landing on the path between Poppy and her sisters.

"Quit acting like a little fool," Lilly scolded.

Poppy's eyes shone with unshed tears. Daisy could see her youngest sister was embarrassed by her clumsiness and humiliated by Lilly's harsh words. The girl's lower lip trembled.

Daisy brushed off Lilly's words. "No squabbling today."

Neither Poppy nor Lilly replied. Poppy still looked like she was on the verge of tears. Lilly looked bored by the girl's display of emotion. Lilly could be as kind as the day was long, or she could be sullen and resentful. It often fell to Daisy to make peace between the two girls.

She spoke to them, determined to keep the mood light. After all, this would likely be their last visit to the lovely springs. "The three of us are part of a secret club."

As she suspected, both girls eyed her with interest. "We are members of an exclusive girls only swim club. We must agree to get along with each other. Be kind. And keep away any male trespassers. No boys allowed. Those are today's rules."

Lilly scoffed.

Poppy gave a tremulous smile. "Girls only?"

"Indeed." Daisy tugged one of Poppy's copper braids. "It's a club. One that doesn't allow boys. Only girls. Only sweet girls." She gave Lilly a pointed look. Lilly rolled her eyes.

Daisy forged on. "And you, Poppy, are the sergeant-at-arms."

Poppy's jaw dropped. Her eyes widened. Softly, she repeated the phrase, *sergeant-at-arms*. Daisy laughed to see how Poppy delighted in the notion of both an exclusive club as well as her special designation.

Poppy giggled. "Poppy Muldoon, Sergeant-at-Arms!"

Lilly groaned audibly but couldn't hold back a smile as they made their way down the path. Poppy skipped ahead, trying her best not to drag Horace's staff. When they reached the spring, Poppy was very careful to set the staff in a safe place by the basket. The girl seemed to be taken with her position in the club as well as her important responsibilities.

The spring day was bright and warm. Daisy couldn't help feeling buoyant and hopeful. Things would work out fine, she told herself. She'd soon find Horace's money. A person could never tell what might come along.

The girls took a blanket from the basket and spread it on a hillock overlooking the water. They'd worn their bathing garments under their dresses. Soon they'd stripped down to the brightly colored, cropped dresses they wore swimming. Uncle Horace hadn't approved of the outfits since the leggings showed off the lower part of their legs, a notion that left him scandalized.

Though he didn't care to swim, he always enjoyed escorting his nieces to the springs. He relished time away from the logging camp and loved venturing out for an afternoon picnic. Just the same, Uncle Horace always grumbled endlessly about young people's notions of propriety.

Daisy smiled as she recalled his exasperation with modern fashions. Her heart felt heavy. Horace had been kind to them at a time when they had no one. She missed him dearly.

Poppy was the first one into the water. Even though the water was warm, she let out a shriek. Lilly followed but didn't screech like Poppy. Instead, she swam gracefully to the far point of the spring and returned a moment later. Lilly was always the graceful swan. Daisy didn't yelp like Poppy, but she winced at the coolness of the water. Water was funny that way. Ten seconds after you got in it felt warm, but at first it could take your breath away.

Daisy eased into the water, pausing on the rocky shoreline to adjust to the temperature.

Poppy mocked her leisurely entry to the pool and flicked water, splashing her.

"You'd better cut that out, Poppy Muldoon." Daisy tried to look stern.

"Or what?" Poppy sassed.

Daisy was about to explain the dire consequences when Poppy dove under the surface and swam away, bobbing up like a little cork on the other side of the spring. The girl grinned impishly as if daring Daisy to come after her.

"You're a rascal," Daisy shouted.

"No, I'm the sergeant-at-arms," Poppy replied.

With that, all three girls laughed. Daisy sighed, knowing she might not hear the end of it for a long while.

They swam for the better part of the morning. Daisy got out first and dried off. Lilly and Poppy both continued swimming while Daisy set out the lunch.

A sound caught her attention. It came from the road leading to Pineville. Her pulse quickened. Her breathing grew shallow as she fought a wave of worry. Who could be riding along this stretch of road at this time of day? She told herself it was nothing. She'd likely imagined the sound, but snatched her uncle's staff, just in case.

An instant later, a rider leading a pack mule came into view.

Chapter Six
Zach Catches Daisy and a Goose Egg

Zach

After three long days on the road, Zach wondered if he might be seeing things. He rubbed his eyes and squinted at the pool of water. Was he truly looking at a group of girls? Three young ladies swimming out here in the lonesome countryside? Or were his eyes playing tricks on him? He'd traveled almost half the state of Texas, seen plenty of interesting sights, but not once had he glimpsed a trio of girls bathing in a spring.

As he drew near, he decided his eyes weren't playing tricks. Moreover, he resolved to stop and say hello, seeing as the young ladies likely lived in Pineville. His attention was drawn to one of them, in particular, a slim girl with honey-color-haired, firmly gripping a stick of some kind while standing in front of a blanket spread for a picnic.

He had no business admiring pretty girls he didn't properly know, and yet he felt drawn to her. He tied his animals to a tree and strolled down the path to the spring. By the time he drew near, the two other girls had scrambled out of the water and hurried to the young lady on the bank.

The girls stood close together, eyeing him warily. They were sisters, surely. They favored each other and wore similar bathing get-ups.

The taller one, the girl he'd admired when he first approached the spring, had a serious demeanor. Thoughtful but ready to defend the other two. Her eyes were blue as a summer sky. From a few paces away, he noted a half-dozen freckles cast across her cheeks.

The stick she held was a walking stick, smooth and strong, but clearly not the usual variety. It was stout and looked like it might give a fellow a headache if need be. As she grew pale, he realized he'd been staring and forced his gaze to the other two, a pair of auburn-haired girls. The older one of the redheads regarded him with a fair degree of alarm.

The younger looked flat-out furious, her youthful face turning a deep scarlet. She snatched the stick from the older girl and held it out as if trying to fend him off. He had to smile at her fierce posture.

"Morning," he said.

Not one replied.

"Are you young ladies from Pineville?"

The eldest, the blonde, nodded.

"I'm Zachary Honeycutt." He offered a cordial smile.

To his surprise, the blonde girl looked distraught. "The owner of the sawmill?"

"Yes, ma'am."

"You intend to stay in the cottage, the one at the end of Mill Road?" she asked.

"Sounds about right." He frowned. "Why do you ask?"

A soft cry of distress fell from her lips. She paled and swayed on her feet as if about to topple over. Why that was, he couldn't imagine. Her face turned white. Zach could tell the blonde gal was going down and moved instinctively. He rushed to her side and caught her just as she sank to the ground.

He felt a jab in his side. The young girl had smacked him with the cane.

"Hey there!" he said, more out of alarm than pain. The young girl backed away.

Zack lifted the girl who'd fainted in his arms, grateful she hadn't fallen to the rocky ground. He also noted a hint of gratitude since he didn't mind holding the pretty girl. Not one bit. The girl was delicate, fragile even. He wondered if she might have gotten too much sun. Sometimes that made folks woozy.

"Something wrong with your sister?" he asked the middle girl.

"No, sir. She's just had a little sinking spell," the girl said quietly. "Daisy's worn out is all. She's always working, you see."

Zach looked down at the girl. Her eyes were closed, and her lashes rested on her pale cheeks.

Daisy...

Her name was Daisy.

He carried her to the blanket spread out on the grass. Gently, he set her down. She wore a bathing dress, one that matched the other girls. Her hair spread around her pretty face, cast out like a sunburst. Her name suited her. Daisy.

He was struck by her in a way he couldn't understand and allowed himself to linger a long moment to admire the girl's delicate features.

"I'm sorry if I upset her," he said mostly to himself.

Something crashed down on his head. A crack sounded next to his ear. Pain shot across his skull. He growled with anger and whirled around to find the small girl standing a few paces away. She wielded the cane, clearly prepared to give him another wallop.

"Leave us alone!" the girl exclaimed.

The middle girl gave a gasp of shock. "Poppy, you little fool. Mr. Honeycutt didn't do anything wrong. Put the mule down."

For the life of him, Zach couldn't imagine what was wrong with these three girls. One had just collapsed. The littlest seemed intent on bashing him with her stick. And the middle girl ranted about a mule. He growled softly, lifting his hand to check the back of his head for blood.

"I said put it down." The middle girl glared at the little one.

"You better get away from my sister." The small girl held the cane behind her, ready to wallop him again.

Zach ran his fingertips over his skull. He found no blood, but he did note a fine goose egg just behind his ear. It had been a while since he'd suffered that sort of injury. Years. Not since he and his brothers had gotten into regular scrapes. The youngest girl had landed a good blow, the little monster.

"I'm not afraid." The pipsqueak took a step closer. "I'll hurt you. I will."

Zach growled. "I'm fixing to hurt *you*, if you don't put that pole down."

Behind him, the older girl moaned softly. Zach suspected she was coming to, but didn't dare turn his back on the small, pint-sized barbarian. She hadn't heeded his warning. If anything, she'd grown bolder, probably because Daisy was stirring, and she intended to protect her.

Zach took four quick steps, reaching the small girl before she could react. He snatched her weapon, then grabbed each end so he could snap it over his knee. Just as he was about to break the cane, Daisy spoke. Her voice was soft, wavering, her words made no sense, but she seemed concerned about the danged stick.

"Don't break it," she murmured.

46

Zach shook his head. He'd hoped that he'd left trouble behind when he left Bethany Springs. The hard travel he'd endured was worth getting away from all the wedding talk. He'd planned to come to Pineville, work hard and enjoy a slight reprieve from all the troublesome womenfolk.

And yet, he hadn't even reached the sawmill and he found more trouble than he could, well, shake a stick at.

The middle girl regarded him with a thoughtful smile, ignoring the other two. She gestured to the basket at her feet. "Would you care for a sandwich, Mr. Honeycutt?"

"All right," he replied hesitantly. He kept a firm grip on the staff. The little girl would need to find another weapon. Zach hoped she wouldn't.

"I'm Lilly," the middle girl said. "Very pleased to meet you."

He nodded.

She brought him a sandwich wrapped in wax paper and motioned for him to sit on the blanket beside Daisy who had managed to sit upright. He didn't question Lilly's instructions. He sat down a respectable distance from Daisy and ate the sandwich, keeping a wary eye on the youngest sister.

"Mr. Honeycutt?" Daisy spoke quietly. "You're certain you'll be staying in the cottage on Mill Road?"

"Yes."

She nodded. He saw her throat move as she swallowed. Something about his reply troubled her deeply.

"Eventually," he added, not quite sure why, but hoping that might ease Daisy's distress. "I might not take up residence for a few days. After all, I've come a little early. The former tenant might still reside in the cottage."

"I see. Well. That's certainly interesting."

The girls seemed to wilt, especially the older two. Upon seeing him eat, the younger one had grabbed a sandwich and was halfway done with it already. *She needs her strength for the next attack*, Zach figured.

He wanted to ask more about the cottage, to find out why the older girls seemed concerned about him moving in, but he held back, not wanting to upset them further.

Daisy rose from the blanket. A moment later, she slipped on a dull brown muslin dress, covering her bathing garment with the ugly material. The other girls had also donned their dresses, covering their swimming garments. They packed their things without speaking, grim and determined expressions etched across their faces.

Zach brushed his fingers across the growing goose egg, wondering where he'd gone wrong. Lord help him. The womenfolk in Pineville were even more bewildering than the females in Bethany Springs.

He got up and slowly folded the blanket he'd been sitting on. None of the girls spoke. They looked weary. Defeated. As if they'd just finished a full day at a sawmill instead of a pleasant morning at the swimming hole.

Daisy took the staff. Lilly took the basket. The youngest polished off the last of her sandwich. The three girls bid him a polite farewell and trudged away, heading down the path to Pineville.

Chapter Seven
Zach Comes to the Cottage

Daisy

Daisy half expected Zach Honeycutt to follow them home. He didn't. Or, at least, not right away. Sensing a reprieve, she returned to her task of searching for the money. The sun sank to the west. She worked without stopping, not caring if the planks broke or remained intact. Both her sisters seemed to sense the urgency. Poppy cried somewhere. Lilly spoke softly, trying to comfort the girl.

The shadows lengthened. Part of her fretted about Mr. Honeycutt's arrival. The other part of her was intent on forging ahead with dogged determination.

Lilly came to the doorway, watching her with concern. "You ought to let me work a while," she said quietly.

Daisy wiped her brow and shook her head.

"Poppy has offered to sell her hair. She heard Mr. Cook talking to one of the mill worker wives and thinks she'll earn top dollar. I could too. The earnings might be enough to pay for a week in a small Pineville cottage, one near the sawmill."

Daisy was too tired to argue.

Lilly went on. "Mr. Cook has always remarked that Poppy and I have a very desirable color of hair."

"Of course, you do," Daisy snapped, tossing the crowbar aside. It landed on the loosened boards with a resounding clatter. "Your hair is lovely. So pretty. I'm sure you've never heard *that* before, have you?"

Silence stretched between the two girls as Daisy's eyes stung with tears. She and Lilly often argued. They argued regularly. But rarely did either sister use a harsh, ugly tone.

Daisy ought to apologize, to offer a conciliatory word, but a hard knot of resistance wrapped around her heart. She was angry. Frightened. And lost. For the first time since her parents died, so very suddenly, she couldn't imagine what the future held for her and her two sisters.

For a long moment, the two girls glared at each other. Finally, Lilly turned away. Daisy listened to her sister's footsteps as she retreated. Lilly hardly ever backed down and here she was, giving up.

Daisy would have enjoyed finding some shred of satisfaction. She found none. Bowing her head, she rubbed her eyes, hoping to quell the tears that threatened. This was not the time for weeping. As the eldest, she bore the responsibility for all three girls.

She heard Poppy talking to someone on the porch. Perhaps someone had come to visit or check on the three sisters. After all, the girls were well-liked in town. They often had visitors pass by to leave a jar of jelly, a basket of eggs or a sack of potatoes.

For some reason, Daisy suspected this visitor was not the type to bring beans or bacon. She held her breath and waited. Silence followed, then the door opened and closed gently. Heavy footfalls echoed across the parlor. They stopped at the hallway. The visitor muttered a few words of dismay before continuing down the hall.

Zach Honeycutt appeared in the doorway. He leaned against the doorframe as he took in the disarray. She expected an outburst. This home belonged to the sawmill, which meant it belonged to his family. He could have made a fuss. She'd hardly blame him. To her surprise, he crossed the room, picked up the crowbar and took over the task of prying up floorboards.

"Daisy," he said quietly.

"Yes, Mr. Honeycutt."

"I don't know what you're doing with his floor, but I'm certain I'm the man to help."

Daisy suppressed a smile and watched as he easily and skillfully removed plank after plank to reveal an empty spot beneath. It was true. He was good at the task. She sighed, resisting the weariness that drifted across her heart. She wasn't sure why he'd taken over her work. It was untoward in a way. In another way, sitting with him was the most natural thing in the world.

She expected a hundred questions, but he didn't ask any. He simply kept working, a wry grin tugging at his lips. Heavens, the man was gallant. Just a few hours before, Poppy had smacked him with Horace's hard staff. Now, he was helping her pry up floorboards, destroying the cabin that belonged to his own family.

Daisy tried to corral her unruly thoughts. Any minute, he could banish her and her sisters from the cottage. What then? There were several families in Pineville that might take them in, but only for a few days. After that, she'd need to devise a whole new plan.

Despite her worries, she managed a few complimentary words about his work. "You do a fine job."

Which sounded absurd.

Mr. Honeycutt plied boards back with hardly any effort. Despite her scattered thoughts, she managed to take note of the empty space beneath each board. No money. None.

Wincing at her own foolishness, she forced her attention away. "You're very skilled, Mr. Honeycutt."

He grinned. "I've done this before."

Her lips tugged to a smile. "You have?"

"My mother built a new house a few years back." Zach tugged up a plank and set it on a neat pile before tackling the next board. "She'd picked out some sort of sensible flooring. Oak, if I recall. Very pretty. Mama was pleased right up until her friend Sophie came to visit. Sophie took one look at the oak floors and wrinkled her nose."

Daisy smiled wearily. "Sophie didn't approve of the oak?"

"Not at all. She declared Mama's floors common and plain."

Daisy could imagine the scene. The Honeycutt family was wealthy. Clearly. Far wealthier than anyone in Pineville. Daisy might have guessed as much. The Honeycutts owned the sawmill, after all. Zach had ridden up on a fine horse and wore clothes he'd probably had made by a tailor.

She glanced at her tattered cuffs and her work-roughened hands.

Tearing her gaze from her callused skin, she tried to imagine Mrs. Honeycutt. In her mind, she pictured a demure, delicate woman with a dozen servants. Zach's mother probably soaked her hands in buttermilk and wore elegant gowns and fine jewels. A lady like Mrs. Honeycutt would look down her nose at the likes of Daisy and her sisters.

Daisy noted a wave of resentment. Just the same, she wanted to know how the story ended. "Did she keep the oak floors?"

Zach snorted. "No. She had them swapped out for some fancy stuff. Thing is, her carpenters quit on her, claiming she was hard to please."

Daisy smiled, imagining Zach's mother reclining on a divan, eating fancy bonbons, ordering the workmen this way and that.

Zach went on. "So, my brothers and I ended up tearing out the oak planks. Mama didn't waste the wood, of course. She used the oak in another ranch house, but she ended up with some fancy wood from Europe for the family's home. Sophie picked it out. When it arrived, my brothers and I were back at work, laying the new floor."

"Was Mrs. Honeycutt satisfied?"

Zach sat back on his heels and set the crowbar aside. "She was."

"And Sophie?"

"Miss Sophie was as satisfied as she'd ever be, I reckon."

He kept his gaze fixed on her. Sitting just a few feet from him, Daisy had the chance to take in his features. Even though she ought to be packing the family's belongings, she allowed herself a moment of foolish admiration.

Zach Honeycutt had a square jaw, one that hadn't seen a razor in a few days, but handsome, nonetheless. He was tanned and his burnished skin contrasted with his sea-blue eyes. He was strong too. His wide shoulders would likely span her doorway.

"So, Daisy Muldoon, tell me something."

A shiver ran down her back. The feeling alarmed her for she'd never had such a response while talking with a gentleman. Zach's voice, a rich baritone, rumbled from the depths of his broad chest and made her heart flutter.

"All right," she replied softly.

"Did someone come visit and tell you that you needed a new floor?"

"No."

"Did you get tired of the scratched wood?"

She shook her head.

"So why are you tearing up the floor of a house that doesn't belong to you?"

Inwardly, she cringed. He could easily and rightfully unleash a storm of anger upon her head. What she was doing was no better than vandalism. Even if she could put each plank back perfectly, she'd broken a fair bit of the wood.

"My great-uncle died," she said.

He knit his brow with sympathy but remained silent, waiting for her to explain more.

"He hid his savings somewhere in this house." She bit her lip as a wave of nervousness swept over her. The disclosure came at a cost. Telling Zach her secret was a risk. He might use the information against her and her sisters.

Zach would be well within his rights to turn her out that very evening. After all, he needed a place to stay. Daisy and her sisters had no claim to the small, sturdy cottage. Not anymore.

In an instant, she pictured a disheartening series of events.

Zach could demand she leave. He'd have plenty of time to track down the money. He could claim the money, taking every penny of her uncle's savings.

At that point, she'd have no recourse. None.

"You sure it's here?" he asked gently.

"I am."

"I'll help you find it then."

She couldn't think of a fitting reply. No words could express her gratitude or her desperate hope.

"I can bed down at the sawmill," he said. "Perhaps I could impose on you for supper in the evenings."

She nodded. "I can bring you lunch too. I sell sandwiches to the loggers several days a week."

"The loggers?" he asked with surprise.

"Yes. It's not much, but I manage to earn a modest income to support my family."

For some reason, this bit of news displeased him. He grumbled under his breath as he tidied the scattered planks and stacked them by the wall. For the life of her, Daisy couldn't imagine why he'd object to her selling sandwiches to the workers. She didn't ask, however. Instead, she kept her mind fixed on the sweet possibility she might be able to save her sisters from a dangerous life in a logging camp.

Chapter Eight
The Sawmill

Zach

Zach returned to the sawmill shortly after nightfall. With a lantern in hand, he made his way up the rickety steps to the office that overlooked operations. The sleeping quarters were primitive. Not as bad as sleeping on the trail during a cattle drive, but a far cry from the comfort of home. The bed was made for a man a head shorter than Zach. As he lay in the narrow cot, his feet hanging over the edge, he tried to ignore the sounds of varmints scurrying along the rafters.

At least they weren't rattlers, he told himself. His thoughts wandered to Daisy and her sisters. Hard to believe he'd only arrived in Pineville that afternoon. Somehow, it seemed as if he'd known Daisy longer. He pictured her, clad in her outlandish swim garment. He'd heard of ladies wearing such get-ups but hadn't been prepared to see the frilly dresses up close.

The fabric only went a short distance past their knees, plainly showing their lower calves and ankles. He felt a wave of warmth rise to his face.

Despite his sheepishness, he smiled at the memory. Daisy could stand to put a little meat on her bones. He was hardly an expert, but he could tell she was a little on the puny side.

Maybe it was on account of her circumstances. He knit his brow. The notion troubled him greatly. She didn't belong here.

He liked the idea of helping her and her sisters find a way to leave the gritty, rough logging camp. He wasn't sure where he'd take her. Someplace where she'd feel safe.

A crash echoed in the mill below. Zach pulled on his boots, lit the lamp, and went downstairs. A man lay sprawled near the back door. He smirked, tried to rise but fell back, unable to get up.

"Who're you?" The man squinted at the lamp and lifted his arm to shield his eyes.

"Zach Honeycutt."

"Oh. The boss man." The stranger struggled to rise but couldn't lift himself more than a few inches before collapsing against the wall.

"You?" Zach asked gruffly.

"Matt Jonas." The man made a sloppy attempt at a salute.

"What are you doing here?"

"Wife's feeling poorly. I'm trying to give her a little peace and quiet."

"Seems you've overindulged."

The man shrugged. "I'm not accustomed to overindulging but my missus is out of sorts."

"You're not sleeping in the mill," Zach explained. "I've bedded down in the office."

The man chuckled. His laugh was interrupted by a lengthy burp. He coughed and tried to sit up, this time managing to get vertical. "Why aren't you sleeping in the cottage?"

"None of your concern."

The man hooted. "Them three girls still there?"

"What's it to you?"

Jonas held up a hand. "You don't need to get sore. No one in Pineville is going to trouble the Muldoon girls."

Zach had to wonder if it was on account of the youngest one. Poppy did a fine job wielding that staff, especially considering the pole was taller than she was. Without thinking, he lifted his hand and gingerly touched the injury she'd given him. It still smarted plenty. He'd have a good-sized lump for a day or two.

"I better not hear about anyone troubling the girls," Zach said gruffly.

"The men sure like when Daisy brings sandwiches."

"She won't be doing that anymore." Zach replied without thinking but didn't feel like changing his response.

"You don't say. Well, the boys will be mighty disappointed."

"Tell the boys to forget about Daisy," Zach growled.

Jonas pulled himself to his feet and swayed precariously. "Ah, heck. No need to fret about the girls. It seems the whole town watches out for them. We don't have too many womenfolk 'round these parts."

"I noticed."

Jonas burped. The burp was smaller than before, but it darned near knocked him off his feet. He chuckled. "Everyone looks out for the three sisters. Even our toughest loggers get stupid when they catch a glimpse of the two older gals. They turn into a bunch of doting biddies when the girls walk by. Course everyone wishes they could court the middle one. Millie, I think her name is."

Zach didn't correct the man. He'd just as soon the men didn't think about the Muldoon girls.

"Or is it Tilly?"

"Close enough," Zach said impatiently.

"Anyway, Old Mr. Cook from the mercantile says he aims to horsewhip any fellow who tries to get fresh."

59

Zack smiled. "I reckon I like the man already."

Jonas stretched and winced with the effort. He stumbled down the dark aisle, heading the direction of the side door. He weaved left and right, bumping against one wall, then lurching to the other, upsetting a stack of pails. They clattered to the floor, rolling lazily across the aisle.

The man continued on his way, hardly noticing the crash of metal. "You'd best get to bed, Mr. Tummyhutt. Morning will be here before you know it."

"Got it. You do the same."

"Right. I'll be in before first light. Need to get the big saw working if we want to keep up with orders."

Zach winced. Jonas would be in no shape to run the big blade. "You'd best check in with me. I might have a few questions about operations."

"You bet, boss. You can count on me."

The man trudged out the door and disappeared into the night. He forgot to close the door behind him. Zach set the buckets out of the way, then shut the door firmly. He looked around the cavernous mill, eyeing the equipment and freshly sawed planks. The lantern cast shadows across the stacks of dried lumber. Zach made a note of looking into flooring for the cottage and made his way back to bed.

In preparation of his trip to Pineville, he'd read everything he could find about sawmills, but he still needed one of the old-timers to show him around. That, he decided, as he tugged off his boots, was a task for the morning.

Chapter Nine
Sister Talk Late at Night

Daisy

For an hour or maybe more, Daisy tossed and turned in bed. Finally, sometime after midnight, she gave up on sleep and got up. The house was quiet. Her sisters slept. As much as she wanted to search for her uncle's money, now was not the time.

She'd have to wait till morning. On second thought, she'd have to wait till the afternoon, since she had several dozen sandwiches to prepare and take to the logging camp.

Fortunately, she had another place to search. Uncle Horace's study. Like all the rooms in the cottage, it was tiny, more of a nook than a room, but it was as good a place as any to hide a sack of money. While she'd already checked the desk several times, she hadn't searched the bookshelves.

Clad in her nightgown and light robe, she picked her way down the hall, trying to avoid making noise. She ran her hands along the desk, groping blindly until she felt the edge of the lamp. She found matches in the top drawer of the desk and lit the lamp. The burning wick cast a soft glow around the small room.

The top shelf held various journals about logging ventures in Texas. She stacked them on one corner of the desk. The next row of books pertained to forestry. She couldn't help smiling as she leafed through the first book, recalling her father's work as an arborist and gardener for a wealthy shipbuilder back in Biloxi.

Father liked to grow trees. Uncle Horace liked to cut them down.

The sound of approaching footsteps drew her attention.

Lilly appeared in the doorway. "What are you doing?" she whispered.

"What do you think I'm doing?" Daisy asked wearily. "The same thing I've been doing since Uncle Horace passed away."

Lilly crossed the room and stopped in front of the desk. She picked a stray volume with a tattered spine. "This is interesting. It's a medical book. I wonder why Uncle Horace had this in his bookshelves."

"Probably because he had to tend to loggers' injuries."

Lilly tilted the book toward the lamp and read for a short spell before flipping through the pages. She drew a sharp breath. "It has several chapters on surgery."

Daisy considered reminding her that Lilly did not like to read. Many times, Lilly would avoid her studies, saying reading was dull, and that girls who read eventually had to wear spectacles, and spectacles ruin a girl's looks.

Lilly tilted the book toward the lamp. "Can't believe all the dreadful subjects in here. Injuries of the hand. Lacerations of the foot. *Gunshot* wounds. Heavens! I hope Uncle Horace never had to take care of a man who'd been shot."

Daisy sighed. "Horace had to tend all sorts of injuries. The nearest doctor is hours away. For that very reason, he read what he could and kept a small medical bag in the hall cabinet."

"I never knew that. I wonder how he learned. Surely not just from reading."

Lilly seemed incredulous, as if doubting that books could impart such valuable skills.

Daisy spoke. "Uncle Horace probably taught himself just like he taught himself how to shoe a horse or repair a broken wagon axle."

Lilly grimaced as she read a passage aloud about parasites. "Ugh," Daisy exclaimed. "I can't stand hearing about illness or injury. The sooner we leave Pineville the better. I'm not sure where we'll go but I'll find a civilized town with a real doctor."

Lilly kept her attention fixed on the book until she reached a firm stopping point.

"Childhood Intestinal Ailments," she exclaimed. With a shudder, she slammed the book shut and shifted her attention to a volume on forestry. She lazily paged through the first chapter, yawned, and set the book aside. "Goodness, it's late. Aren't you taking lunch to the men in the morning?"

"I am. But I can't fall asleep."

"You'll be so tired, Daisy-Maisy."

Daisy smiled at the old endearment and replied with one just for her younger sister. "I know, Lilly-Milly."

"Why can't you sleep?"

"I don't know. I need to catch a few winks. I've got a long day. After I take lunch to the workers, I need to cook a nice dinner since Mr. Honeycutt's coming to eat with us."

Lilly lifted several books from the shelf and started a new stack on the desk. "Would you like me to take the lunches? That way, you could rest a spell, or start on dinner."

"I don't think that's a good idea," Daisy said gently. "I don't want you mingling with those men. Most of them are sweet on you. Or so it seems."

"You mean to tell me that you intend to hide me away. Keep me out of sight till I'm an old woman?"

In the dim light, Daisy couldn't make out her sister's expression but heard the smile behind her words.

Daisy nodded. "Seems as though that might be-"

Lilly stopped her with an upraised hand. "Don't tell me. Prudent?"

"Well, yes. I was about to say just that. It's not your fault that you're a lovely, pleasant-looking young lady. I simply want to avoid the problems that men might cause you. Men come and go at these logging camps. Pineville seems peaceful now, but you never know when a troublemaker might arrive."

Lilly didn't reply. She turned silently near the door. Daisy kept working. Suddenly, she sensed her sister's attention fixed on her. She glanced up from her task to find Lilly watching, her lips curved with the barest hint of a smile.

"What?" Daisy demanded.

"How come you're so sure the men don't find *you* pleasing?"

"Because I'm just a plain girl, especially when I'm standing beside you."

Lilly snickered.

A flicker of irritation sparked inside Daisy's thoughts. They'd had this conversation a number of times before, so Daisy couldn't imagine what Lilly found amusing. She ignored her sister as she finished clearing the second shelf.

"You're the only one who describes yourself as plain," Lilly said.

"Well, I am. Plain."

Lilly gave her a doubting look.

"It's perfectly obvious," Daisy said, struggling to hide her irritation. "Young men hardly give me a second glance, not when they can look at you with their puppy-dog eyes. It doesn't bother me. Not for my sake, anyway. I simply want to shield you from untoward attention."

Lilly sank into a nearby chair, rested her elbows on the armrest and steepled her fingers as she considered Daisy's words. Daisy couldn't imagine what her sister found so interesting. Anyone with eyeballs could see the truth of what Daisy said. She narrowed her eyes at Lilly. The look earned her a sunny smile from her sister.

Daisy shoved a stack of books to one side. "Would you care to explain what's so blasted funny now?"

Lilly giggled. "I'm fairly certain *one* particular gentleman finds you pleasing."

Daisy blinked. Heat rushed to her face. She pressed her lips together and kept on with her task. Lilly was a flibbertigibbet. If Daisy showed any sign of dismay, Lilly would give her no end of grief. She'd poke fun at her morning, noon, and night. The last thing Daisy wanted was Lilly teasing her in front of Mr. Honeycutt.

Lilly's grin widened. "He hardly takes his eyes from you."

Daisy refused to pay her sister a bit of attention. She gathered a half-dozen books on flowering plants and set them by the forestry volumes. Next, she tackled the lower shelf which held an assortment of schoolbooks for Poppy, books that hadn't been touched since Uncle Horace had passed.

Lilly leaned forward, resting her chin on her hand, a smile playing on her lips.

"Mr. Honeycutt rushed to your side when you swooned this afternoon. I thought that was terribly romantic. I won't ask your opinion since your eyes rolled back as he caught you. You probably don't remember what if felt like to be held in his arms."

Daisy remembered.

She remembered *perfectly*. Normally, she prided herself on her fortitude. She'd never, ever fainted before. She wondered if Lilly was right about her eyes rolling back and cringed inwardly. Why couldn't she have appeared a little more feminine and perhaps even alluring?

One thing was certain, she'd likely never again find herself in the arms of such a handsome man. Which was fine. Perfectly fine. She reminded herself that she was the sensible sister, not the sister who prided herself on being an expert at flirting.

Despite Daisy's best intentions, she couldn't keep her lips from tugging into a foolish smile. The memory drifted back, the way his strong arms wrapped around her so protectively. Mr. Honeycutt was strapping and strong and kind and noble.

A small sigh escaped her lips. She grew flustered, bracing herself for a round of teasing from Lilly. Thankfully, Lilly didn't notice her response. She seemed to be mulling over an important issue, judging from her thoughtful expression.

"I'm going to have to think about this," Lilly said, her tone solemn. She tapped her temple and knit her brow. "I'll have to find a way to protect my pleasant-looking sister from Mr. Honeycutt's lingering gaze."

She shook her head, giving a look of mock alarm. "What if Mr. Honeycutt is the very troublemaker that you've always fretted about?"

Before Daisy could silence her sister, Lilly rose from the chair and took a few steps to the doorway where she turned to face Daisy. "I'll need to supervise matters. Closely. Above all, I can't leave you two alone."

"Oh, hush," Daisy muttered. She didn't want to play into Lilly's teasing, but her curiosity burned inside her. "Why can't you leave the two of us alone?"

"Don't you know?" Lilly spoke airily. "It wouldn't be *prudent*."

She darted away before Daisy could come back with a teasing comment of her own. Lilly hurried to her room as her playful laughter drifted across the nighttime quiet. A moment later, her door closed softly.

Chapter Ten
Better to Fire Him Than Hurt Him

Zach

Waking in the predawn darkness, Zach needed a moment to figure out where he was. It wasn't his cabin, nor was it his mother's guest room. He wiped the sweat from his brow. Bad dreams had tormented him. Fire. Smoke. And then it came to him. He was in Pineville, in the office of the sawmill. He'd come to East Texas to look in on the new venture, to learn how things were done and decide if it was a venture worth keeping.

The dream likely stemmed from last year's fire that had burned part of the mill and a dozen or so acres of the nearby forest. The fire caused the owner to default on his bank loan. Since Zach's mother owned the bank, she'd acquired the mill.

She didn't want it. It was too far away from home and lately all she wanted was to be a grandmother. Which was how Zach ended up sleeping on an undersized cot in the mill office.

His thoughts cleared. It all came back to him now, mixed with a few snippets of his fake engagement to Marie.

He winced.

He didn't want to think about how Marie had tricked him or why he'd gone along with the farce. Probably because he always tried to help out Marie and the McCord family any time he could.

Scrubbing his hand down his face, he pushed thoughts of the dilemma aside. He'd rather think about the pretty young lady he'd held in his arms just yesterday. He lay in the darkness and smiled, thinking about Daisy Muldoon.

Daisy...

His smile widened. He pictured her pretty face and recalled her sweet smile. What was she doing right then? Sleeping? He hoped so. It was too early to be up. He'd get up anyway, he decided, throwing the blankets aside. If he rose early, he'd have time to look over the mill before the supervisor arrived.

If he were back in Bethany Springs, he'd already be up, saddling his horse and heading out before dawn to tend to the Honeycutts' vast herds of Longhorns. Working as a cowboy suited him. It was the only type of life he'd ever imagined. He'd rather be outdoors on the range any day, especially when compared to spending his day inside a dusty, noisy sawmill.

It couldn't be helped. If Mama needed a hand with a family business, he wanted to be first in line to offer. Especially since his brothers had both recently married.

One thing was certain, Zach didn't want his mother working in a logging town. Pineville was no place for a lady, which was why it galled him to think of Daisy and her sisters living alone in the cottage.

He splashed water over his face and dressed. His stomach rumbled. Without a kitchen, there was little he could do about hunger pangs. He'd eaten the last of the provisions he'd packed for the trip.

For now, he'd keep his attention fixed on his first day on the job. Later, he'd figure out how to get a bite to eat. Maybe he'd find a boarding house or lunch counter. He made an attempt to comb his hair, albeit without a mirror. He tossed the comb aside and put on his cowboy hat.

Downstairs, the first mill workers wandered into the shop as the sun lit the horizon. None of the men, aside from Matt Jonas, knew he was the owner's son, which suited him fine. It would allow him a chance to see how things ran when a superior wasn't around.

An oxcart laden with immense pine logs rumbled up to the back door. The bullwhacker guided the animals into position. "C'mon, boys," he urged good-naturedly. "It's a brand-new day. Not time for a nap. Step lively, Roscoe."

The animals strained against their yokes and slowly pulled the cart up the last incline to the side of the shop. A team of men met the cart and prepared to unload the logs. They worked quickly while the driver leaned against the doorway and offered cheerful insults to both the workers and his animals.

With a deafening crash, the logs tumbled to the floor of the shop. A moment later, the oxcart was headed back down the ramp. Several men worked together to ease the first log to a trolley. They pushed it to the back where another worker had fired up one of the saws.

The roar of the steam-powered saw shook the mill. The giant timbers supporting the walls and roof trembled from the reverberations. The sheer power of the immense saw made the scatter of wood shavings jump on the floor planks.

Zach watched as the men cut the first log into even planks. The sharp blade sliced the wood like a hot knife through butter. The scent of fresh pine wafted through the shop along with swirling motes of sawdust. By the time the saw operator finished the first log, the men brought a second. The freshly cut wood was prepared for the kiln where it would be dried and cured.

71

The men worked swiftly, never stopping. Zach marveled at the entire operation. While he'd always considered cowboying hard work, he had to admit working in a timber mill might be every bit as taxing.

Just after daybreak, Matt Jonas entered the mill, looking a little sheepish. "Sorry I'm late, boss. Guess I shoulda mentioned I'm the supervisor. I took over when Horace Muldoon passed away."

Zach narrowed his eyes. "You always show up late?"

"No, sir. I'm mighty sorry about last night."

"You better be. If I smell whiskey on your breath again, I'll fire you."

The man nodded. "You can count on me, sir."

"That's what you said last night. When you could barely stand."

Jonas winced. "Won't happen again. I can guarantee it. See, my mother-in-law was visiting. She always leaves my wife out of sorts on account of fussing about everything."

Zach didn't reply. He wasn't sure if there was a good answer to that sort of comment. One thing was certain. The Honeycutt cowboys never started the day talking about mother-in-law troubles.

Jonas laughed nervously. "The good news is she's leaving today. My mother-in-law I mean. Not my wife."

Zach narrowed his eyes.

Jonas waved his hands. "I won't touch a drop, I swear. Not a single drop. Not till my mother-in-law visits this time next year."

Zach sighed and shook his head. "I'll hold you to it, Jonas."

From that point on, Matt Jonas showed that he knew a great deal about the timber business. Everything from felling trees to transport and running a sawmill. As the morning wore on, he grew steadier and took on an air of authority.

"You seem to know your stuff," Zach remarked.

"Mr. Muldoon taught me a great deal. I only worked under him a couple of months before he passed, but he was a fine man. Fair. Hard-working. Intelligent. I only wished I'd known him longer."

Zach instantly thought of Daisy and her earnest, serious demeanor. That sort of good character had to be something of a family trait amongst the Muldoons. He felt certain the girls followed in their family footsteps.

"We've only got about twenty men on the payroll right now," Jonas said as they walked the short path to the logging site.

"I saw that in the report."

Jonas looked apologetic. "It's hard to find and keep good men. And when we do, we usually lose one or two a month."

"They quit?"

"Some. Others get injured and then quit. It takes time to bring a new man along, to teach them how we do things at the mill. We've got the lowest injury rate of anyone around and that's on account of teaching folks how things are done."

After a spell, Zach and Jonas came to a stop at the edge of the pine trees. The woodland grew thick in every direction, rising up from the forest floor. Wind stirred across the branches. The trees swayed gently. As Zach traveled to Pineville, he'd noticed the wind as it moved through the trees. He'd found the sound pleasing but heard none of that soothing hush as he stood with Matt Jonas.

What he heard was the steady hum of activity, the busy work of the lumberjacks and loggers.

Oxcarts moved down the trail, hauling heavy piles of timber. Empty carts rumbled up the trail, ready for the next load. Men shouted to each other as they worked. Every so often, they'd yell a warning to their companions, alerting them to the danger of a falling tree. In the next instant, an immense pine would crash to the ground.

Zach watched the nearest team of loggers, working a few paces from where he and Jonas stood. The two men worked in tandem, sawing the trunk of a pine tree. Zach couldn't help feeling sorry for the young men. They wore shirtsleeves, no jackets. Despite the cool spring morning, their shirts were drenched. Zach lifted his gaze to the top of the tree.

"Don't worry, Mr. Honeycutt. The tree will fall the other way."

"I'm not worried."

Zach whistled to the loggers. They stopped sawing.

"You boys mind if I try working that saw?"

"No, sir," they replied.

One of the men backed away. His partner gestured to the handle of the long blade. Zach put on a pair of gloves and grasped the wooden grip. He tried to work in tandem with the other fellow but his first attempts to use the saw failed badly. His partner offered an encouraging smile.

It ought to have been easier to run a saw back and forth, Zach thought to himself.

After a dozen tries, he and the other fellow managed to find a rough cadence. The long saw bit through the wood. Sawdust flew. The scent of pine wafted through the air. The cut deepened. Slowly. The work proved slow and arduous. This was as hard as riding a bronc or roping a passel of ornery yearlings. Finally, they sawed the width of the immense pine, or close enough. The tree teetered, swayed, and fell to the ground.

The sky opened above, offering a patch of sunshine. As much as Zach preferred wide open sky, he couldn't help feeling a little sad about the loss of the majestic tree.

"Mighty hard work." Zach said to the men. "How long do you boys work like this? Seems mighty taxing."

"Dawn till dark. Just like the rest of the men."

Zach nodded and bid the men farewell. He and Jonas walked back to the sawmill, talking along the way. Jonas spoke of the loggers as well as the sawmill workers.

"We boast a fine crew. They work hard and risk life and limb."

"I believe every word," Zach said.

Zach went straight to the office to write a brief letter to his mother. After a few preliminaries, he explained that the mill seemed to be in good working order. The timber in the surrounding area ought to hold out for years to come, a blessing, considering most mills only remained in business a few short years before having to pick up and move.

He left the more pertinent matters till the end.

The men work tirelessly. According to the manager, he struggles to find workers because so many mills are hiring. It would be in our interest to offer workers a shorter workday for the same wage. I believe the mill would be as productive since the men wouldn't be worn out. The work is brutal. Most of the men look spent and haggard.

I plan to shorten their days from eleven hours to nine. I intend to keep their pay the same. The mill is showing a good profit. We have the money and I'd like to invest in the fine men working here.

All my best,

Zachary.

He tucked the note into an envelope and directed one of the shop helpers to take the letter to the Pineville post office.

Zach felt a sense of relief but still had a full morning. A new director was on his way to the mill, a man who could advise Zach on how to improve production. Zach paced the floor as he waited. While Zach didn't much feel like chatting with the fella, he had to oblige his mother. After all, Mama had gone through heck and high water to get the man to hire on with her mill.

Zach wasn't sure why the man was considered such a fine addition to the mill. Mama hadn't explained her reasons too well. She'd paid the man a small fortune and he was on his way.

Arthur Rankin. Some sort of up-and-coming forestry expert. A man who'd trained on the West Coast in addition to working for a big outfit in Pennsylvania. Mama had acted like the man had *invented* lumber. He'd be able to steer the company to new contracts and rise above so many of the other mills in the area.

Mr. Rankin strolled into the mill office ten minutes past the appointed time. Zach didn't complain. He could see right off that Rankin had a high opinion of himself. He set his satchel down, hung his hat on a nearby hook and proceeded to give a long-winded report about his travels to Texas.

Trains. Wagons. Delays. More trains.

Zach tried to hide his impatience. No cowboy would ever carry on like Rankin. The man was molasses in January and Zach was more than eager to be done with this meeting with the stuffed shirt.

Zach missed more than a few words of Rankin's story. Thoughts of Daisy kept getting in the way. She would come to town soon. She'd bring her basket, ready to sell her wares to the hungry workmen. First, she'd visit Zach, however. Zach had made sure of that last night when he left the cottage, insisting she drop by the mill office so he could buy a sandwich.

That wasn't the real reason Zach wanted to see Daisy. He yearned to talk to her for the simple reason that he enjoyed her company. The notion might have struck him as peculiar if Rankin hadn't been droning on about the final leg of his endless journey.

"I'm happy I finally found my way," Mr. Rankin concluded with a chuckle, his back turned to Zack as he looked out the window.

"So am I, Mr. Rankin," Zach said. "I'm hopeful you'll help increase profits the first year. I'm eager to win some of the railroad contracts to supply ties for the new lines they're proposing."

Rankin nodded, keeping his gaze fixed on some spot out the window. "If anyone can turn things around, it's me," he said absently.

Zach didn't need the man to turn things around so much as add to the already good profits. He shuffled through a stack of papers, searching for the last earnings report. In a moment of carelessness, he sent a jar of pencils off the side of the desk. They hit the floor with a crash. Rankin hardly noticed.

Zach ignored the mess. Instead of tidying the scattered pencils, he shoved them under his desk with the toe of his boot. With a few well-chosen words, he heaved a deep sigh. He'd spent less than a day in the cramped office and already he'd made a fine mess.

He was a cowboy, accustomed to wide open spaces. Not a fellow suited to sitting at a desk and listening to windbags. He only halfway listened to Mr. Rankin go on about something that held his attention.

"Now that's a mighty sweet sight," Rankin murmured.

Zach looked up. "What do you mean by that? A sweet sight?"

Rankin drew a deep sigh, keeping his gaze fixed on a spot somewhere on the road below. "That pretty little piece of fluff."

Zach frowned.

Rankin went on. "She's likely some little lightskirt, a local girl."

Zach's throat tightened. He waited, wondering what Rankin was going on about. Surely not...

"Hard to know," the man said. "Here in the logging towns, folks come and go. Especially the lower-class workers and their families. Just the same, I'd sure like to get acquainted."

Rankin's unsavory tone sent a surge of anger along Zach's veins. He remained still, a few paces from the renowned expert. Zach clenched his jaw and bided his time. Without asking, he knew exactly who Rankin was watching. There was no question.

Zach knew.

Rankin watched Daisy. He was watching her and saying filthy things about her. Calling her a lightskirt. Lower-class. Daisy. *His* Daisy.

"I do have a soft spot for blondes," Rankin said.

Zach moved to the window and just as he suspected, Daisy approached the sawmill. She carried a heavy basket and wore a cheerful smile. Meanwhile, Rankin watched with a predatory glint in his eye.

Zach noted a surge of protective instincts, so strong they took him by surprise. Daisy was so innocent, so vulnerable.

She couldn't know that a man watched her walking to the sawmill. Zach held his tongue, barely. Somehow, he kept his composure. His anger subsided enough for him to speak.

"Mr. Rankin, you're fired. Get out of my sawmill."

Chapter Eleven
Zach Buys the Whole Basket

Daisy

She was running late. As usual. Even though she set out early, she'd stopped to visit along the way. The folks of Pineville were kind and generous and neighborly, especially since Uncle Horace passed away. By the time she arrived at the mill, she'd received several kind offers for her and her sisters.

Mrs. Cook, the wife of the mercantile owner, promised to send a loaf of sourdough. Mrs. Duke would send a basket of new potatoes. Mrs. Dalton insisted on giving her several jars of apple butter.

Daisy had to admit everyone had treated her with tremendous kindness in the last few months. Uncle Horace liked to brag about Pineville. He claimed he'd never lived in a nicer mill town and that was saying something.

She stepped inside the sawmill. It was humming with activity. The large saw in the middle, taller than she was, was screeching loudly as it cut through the trunk of a pine tree, an oxcart rattled away after unloading three more logs outside, men shouting, young fellows sweeping up the sawdust that lay everywhere. Daisy nodded a silent greeting to a few of the men she'd seen before and made her way to the mill office.

Just as she set her boot on the lowest stair, the office door slammed with a bang. Daisy's eyes widened. A portly man hurried down the stairs and rushed past. She watched as he raced out of the mill as if chased by a horde of wild animals.

For a long moment, she considered if she ought to go up the stairs. Perhaps Mr. Honeycutt was in a foul mood or in the midst of some important and trying negotiation. Maybe she ought to wait. What if Mr. Honeycutt turned on her and raged, frightening her in the very same way he'd frightened the man fleeing the sawmill.

She considered her options. She could simply leave and forget that he'd asked her to stop by. Or she could venture up to his office. If nothing else, she could offer him a sandwich. With a deep breath, she gathered her courage, went up the narrow stairs and let herself inside the office.

Mr. Honeycutt stood by the window, arms folded, glaring at her with a fierce fire in his eyes.

She swallowed hard and set her basket down. "Hello."

"Hello," Mr. Honeycutt replied.

"The man who just left." She pointed to the door, trying to find the right words. "Well, you see. He ran down the stairs as if he was frightened of something... something quite terrible."

"Is that so?" His eyes held hers. "Good."

She tried to find a reasonable response but failed, so she remained silent.

"Did he speak to you?"

Daisy shook her head. Why would the man speak to her? "I hope I'm not interrupting." She clasped the basket handle. "I could come back if you like."

"No. Don't go."

Glancing around the dingy office, she glimpsed a narrow cot pushed against the far wall. "Is that where you slept?"

He gave a curt nod.

"Oh, dear." She smiled tentatively. "That explains a lot. It's no wonder you're out of sorts. I imagine you haven't even had breakfast. Poppy gets quite irritable when she's had a poor night of sleep. And she's hardly able to speak civilly if she skips breakfast. I tell you, it's a little frightening. Though on second thought, I think you understand perfectly, judging from your scowling expression."

Mr. Honeycutt didn't reply.

She pulled back the linen covering the basket. "Let's see. I have ham. Ham and cheese. Egg salad and roast beef. Usually, I don't offer beef, but Mr. Cook gave me a good price. I'd be happy to give you one of each before I take my wares to the workers. I'm sure they're all waiting in that spot under the trees on the other side of the mill."

"Leave the basket," he said gruffly as he crossed the room, stopping before her.

"The basket. The whole basket?"

"Right. The whole basket."

She laughed nervously, unsure of what he meant. When he stood so close, she couldn't think clearly. Her thoughts drifted to matters she ought to ignore, like the span of his shoulders or his enticing, masculine scent. Mr. Honeycutt was a little rough around the edges. He could do with a shave. His shirt needed a little time with a hot iron, but aside from a few housekeeping details, she noted, not for the first time, that Mr. Honeycutt was as handsome a man as she'd ever seen. Ever.

"I'm buying the whole basket," he said. "Leave it with me. I'll bring it this evening."

"My word," she marveled. "You are hungry, aren't you?"

Mr. Honeycutt didn't laugh or even smile. "I don't want you mixing with those fellows."

Her heart thudded. There'd been a time when she'd been afraid to sell her wares to the loggers. She'd heard the stories. Mr. Cook warned her that plenty of men who drifted through logging camps weren't any good at all. But nothing had happened. What was more, she needed the money she earned from selling lunches.

"I'll pay you," Mr. Honeycutt said as if reading her mind. "I'll compensate you for every one of the sandwiches. And more."

"That's ridiculous," she said. "I don't want to be beholden to you."

He shrugged a shoulder, kept his gaze on her as he took a sandwich from the basket.

She lifted her chin. "I intended to use the money to pay for provisions at the mercantile this afternoon."

"Charge the bill to the Honeycutt account."

She recoiled. And how would that look exactly, she wanted to ask. She could almost imagine Mr. Cook's shock when she announced she wouldn't be paying for her purchases. That he should send the bill to the owner of the sawmill. Poor Mr. Cook would be struck speechless, as would any other shoppers in the mercantile.

Meanwhile, Mr. Honeycutt gave her a look that was even more angered than before. A small pulse drummed on his temple. He kept his steely gaze fixed on her.

She regarded him thoughtfully, refusing to be cowed by the dark look in his eyes. She also tried to keep from noting his enticing scent and rumpled hair. What would happen if she brushed a few locks aside? She didn't dare give the notion another thought.

Was it just yesterday when he'd scooped her up in his strong arms? She eyed his sturdy build and wondered how a man could be so tender one day and so disagreeable the next. She gave him a prim, disapproving look, one that seemed to have no effect at all.

All she could say for certain was that she needed her basket, no matter what he said about the matter.

Mr. Honeycutt took a bite of the sandwich, hardly pausing to chew before tearing off another bite. Daisy watched with dismay. The man ate as if he was, for some reason, angry at the poor, defenseless sandwich.

He seemed put out with her as well.

She glanced at her basket and wondered if he disapproved of her small venture. He'd said as much the night before. Why would he want to keep her from working?

"This is absurd," Daisy said, speaking mostly to herself as she took her bonnet from the basket.

Mr. Honeycutt didn't reply.

She put the bonnet on and tied the ribbons. "You can return the basket after you've eaten the sandwiches. All twenty-four of them. I need to be on my way. I have to do a little shopping before I go home. I look forward to seeing you this evening."

She didn't *really* look forward to seeing him. In truth, she worried about his visit. What if he came to eat with her and her family while still simmering with the same bad mood? She always tried to shield her sisters from rough elements and wondered if she'd unwittingly invited a particularly rough element to her home to share supper.

Another worry tugged at her thoughts. What if Mr. Honeycutt came to her home this evening and announced that she and her sisters needed to leave? Soon. After a night on the narrow, too-short cot, he likely yearned for better lodgings. This had to be the reason for his bad mood.

"I need to pay for the basket of sandwiches," he said gruffly.

"We can discuss it some other time." She wanted to add *when you're not growling like a bear.*

She held her tongue and without another word, turned on her heel and left Mr. Honeycutt's office. She chided herself as she made her way down the narrow stairs. It had been a mistake to dwell on Mr. Honeycutt's kind concern or any romantic notions. She ought to have ignored the way his eyes held hers as he spoke or the deep timbre of his voice. None of it mattered. Not one bit. No, he was every bit as unpredictable and irascible as all the other men in Pineville.

Daisy marched past the mill workers, down the wide dusty aisle and through the front doorway without so much as a backward glance.

Chapter Twelve
Zach Reveals Something Important

Zach

Pacing his office, Zach seethed, furious with himself. He wasn't one to lose his temper. Everyone knew he was the kindhearted, thoughtful Honeycutt. Or so he liked to think. He tried to work back through the morning's events to understand why or how he'd lost his temper. It had happened so quickly. Just a few comments from Rankin had set him off.

The crude words infuriated him, but why?

He'd heard plenty of rough talk before. For some reason, this time the coarse words had offended him. Deeply. There had to be one single reason. It was on account of Daisy. The coarse words were directed at a girl he cared about.

Daisy.

The realization struck him with a jolt of surprise. He stopped pacing. Standing in the middle of the sawmill office, he grappled with the astonishing notion. He cared for Daisy Muldoon. He cared for her. Deeply. It was true. He cared for a girl he'd only just met.

It made no sense to him. For some reason, it seemed impossible. A vague, nagging worry troubled him. He knew there were a heap of reasons why he shouldn't have a soft spot in his heart for Daisy. It was true. What was more, there was a very important reason he ought to forget about the girl. What was it exactly?

And then it dawned on him.

He, Zach Honeycutt, was engaged. To Marie. Not that he or Marie had any intention of exchanging vows. He understood that he merely played a part in Marie's scheme to travel. Still, guilt stung his conscience.

He needed to find Daisy and apologize for his manners. He ought to confess, tell her he was engaged. Clear his conscience. Yes. That was the right thing to do. Rubbing the back of his neck, he considered how that sort of confession might sound. Probably a little peculiar.

I'm engaged to a childhood friend. Neither of us actually want to walk down the aisle and exchange vows. No. Marie simply wanted to travel. Peculiar? Yes. And yet, that's how I ended up engaged.

He grimaced. It sounded dubious. Regardless, he needed to tell Daisy he was sorry for his behavior. Striding from the office and down the narrow stairs, he remembered the basket of sandwiches. He returned to the office, snatched the basket, and went back down the stairs. One of the workmen was just stepping out of the tool room. He carried a freshly sharpened pickaroon.

Zach gave him the basket.

The worker's eyes widened. "What's this, sir?"

"Sandwiches."

"Sandwiches?"

"You heard me. Share them with the rest of the men."

Zach left the mill and turned in the direction of the mercantile. As he passed the blacksmith shop, he caught sight of Daisy. He drew a deep breath. Just the sight of her gave him a comforting sense of calm. She walked with a purposeful stride but one he easily overcame. He caught up with her just as she got to the entrance of the mercantile.

"Daisy," he called from a few paces back.

She turned around with a look of surprised dismay. "Mr. Honeycutt."

"I wanted to speak to you."

Her expression softened as her eyes sparked with amusement. "Would you like me to bring you some more sandwiches?"

Frowning, he shook his head. "No, thank you."

An older man stepped past them on the walkway and tipped his hat to Daisy. "Hello Miss Muldoon. I've received the book you ordered. Be sure to stop by the shop when you get a chance."

She smiled. "Thank you, Mr. McDonald."

The man gave Zach a pointed look as he continued past.

Zach wondered why the stranger might disapprove of him. He didn't have long to consider the question. A couple came from the other direction and thanked Daisy for the meal she'd sent while the husband recovered from some illness. The young man and woman both gave Zach a stern look as they went on their way.

The shopkeeper was the next person to give Zach a hard look. He came to the doorway and crossed his arms as he glared at Zach. "Everything all right, Miss Daisy?"

"Thank you, Mr. Cook. I'm just visiting with Mr. Honeycutt, the new owner of the sawmill."

Mr. Cook didn't seem a bit impressed with the notion of meeting the new owner of the sawmill, judging by his deeply furrowed brow. Zach held out his hand and offered a polite greeting. The shopkeeper took it reluctantly and gripped Zach's hand with a too-firm grasp.

Zach understood the meaning clearly.

Stay away from Daisy Muldoon...

89

Mr. Cook excused himself and returned to his shop, leaving Zach and Daisy on the mercantile stoop.

"I wanted to apologize," Zach said hurriedly before anyone else stopped to stare daggers at him.

"For what?" Daisy smiled as she loosened the ties of her bonnet.

Zach watched her as she tugged the bonnet from her head. Just then a soft breeze blew, lifting a delicate strand of her golden hair. The strand waved and danced across her pretty face as Daisy tried to brush it aside. The breeze toyed with the loose tress, making it impossible for Daisy to capture the unruly strand of hair.

He felt a strong urge to brush the hair from her face. His fingers itched to touch that delicate strand. Somehow, he resisted. Instead, he crossed his arms and tried to remind himself to act like a gentleman, not a rash, impolite schoolboy.

"Why do you want to apologize?" Daisy asked.

Zach tried to remember. The breeze died down, thankfully. The air stilled around them, allowing the loose strand to slowly drift down to the pale expanse of her neck.

"Mr. Honeycutt?"

He shook his head. "Sorry. Yes, well, I wanted to tell you that I'm engaged to be married."

Her smile faded. A fragile wounded look flashed behind her eyes. It vanished just as quickly, however.

"Congratulations," she replied.

"What I want to say is that the situation is a tad awkward."

"It's none of my concern, Mr. Honeycutt."

"I'd like to explain a few things."

Daisy flushed, her cheeks turning a soft hue of pink. "There's nothing to explain."

"But there is. It's a bit of a long story."

"Please, Mr. Honeycutt," she spoke softly, her voice edged with alarm. "I don't care to hear any of this. Especially not in the middle of town. Pineville is rife with gossips."

Glancing around, Zach quickly understood what she meant. The blacksmith stood in his doorway, giving him a threatening look. Other townsfolk had stopped to stare and eyed him with suspicion. Daisy appeared distressed and they blamed him. Rightfully.

Zach had made a mess of things and clearly Daisy was mortified.

"Of course, Daisy. I didn't mean to insult or offend."

She drew her shoulders back and offered a small, polite smile. "If you'll excuse me, I have to shop for dinner this evening."

"I could wait for you and walk you home."

"I don't think that would be prudent, Mr. Honeycutt."

Unsure what more to say, Zach held the shop door open for her. She eyed him with a cool expression, clearly unwilling to forgive him for his clumsy attempt to confess and apologize. He'd try again later at dinner, maybe even rehearse his words a time or two so he'd get it right. He needed to pay for the basket of sandwiches too.

He gestured to the open door, unsure why she seemed reluctant to pass.

"Thank you," she said primly. Lifting her chin, she stepped inside the mercantile where she was greeted by several shoppers.

Chapter Thirteen
Poppy Finds a Treasure

Daisy

Mr. Cook insisted on taking her home on the mercantile buckboard. The mercantile owner was a kindly gentleman, but his concern for Daisy and her sisters came with a generous serving of unhelpful advice.

"That little Poppy ought to be in school," he advised as they drove the short distance to the cottage. "She's a right smart girl."

"Thank you," Daisy said, trying not to sound resentful. "I agree. Unfortunately, Pineville doesn't have a school. So, I'm not sure where I ought to send her."

"Horace told me you intended to teach her, that you were bringing books and whatnot."

"True. I did bring books." Daisy rubbed her forehead. "I have to confess that I haven't kept up with her lessons."

"My sister has a school in Louisiana. A boarding school for girls. She often takes in students who show promise. I could write her if you like."

Daisy drew a sharp breath. "No!"

Mr. Cook knit his brow. "I only meant to help. I know you've struggled since Horace passed."

"It's true but I'd never want to part from my sisters. Never."

"Suit yourself. But if you ever change your mind, I'm sure that Agnes would welcome Poppy." He chuckled. "Even if she is a little pip. Did I tell you she keeps asking for me to sell puppies and kittens? She likes to say that would make my mercantile first-rate."

Any other time, Daisy might have laughed at Mr. Cook's story about Poppy. Her little sister often made her laugh, but his story only made her feel tired. So tired. Yes, she knew that Poppy needed lessons. She also knew that her little sister would dearly love a puppy or kitten.

Her thoughts drifted to Zach's confession. He was engaged. She shouldn't care, but she did. She chided her foolish heart for caring. It was absurd, especially when she had so many other troubles that needed her attention.

Lilly and Poppy met her at the road. Mr. Cook unloaded her purchases, handing them to the girls before bidding them farewell. A moment later, the buckboard rumbled down the road.

"We made daisy chains," Poppy said. "While you were in town."

Daisy noted the crowns on her sisters' heads. Poppy's lay crooked. Lilly's sat perfectly a top her head. Of course, it did. Daisy noted that the flowers weren't even daisies. They didn't look remotely like daisies. They were a type of flower called winecups and they weren't white and yellow. They were a pale purple with delicate, silken petals. Nothing like the sturdy daisy.

Poppy was so happy about the crowns that Daisy didn't want to correct her.

"I'm thinking of taking a job," Lilly announced as they unpacked the purchases.

"No, you're not," Daisy replied.

"Don't you want to know what it is?" Lilly asked.

"I do not. We're not staying in Pineville."

"Mr. Tilson plans to quit logging and open a saloon. He claims he could make a fortune."

"A saloon?" Daisy asked. "You didn't really just say that word, did you?"

Lilly looked affronted.

"What's a saloon?" Poppy asked.

"It's a disreputable place," Daisy answered. "No self-respecting woman would work in a saloon."

Poppy wrinkled her nose. "Are we poor? I could sell my hair."

"We're not poor," Daisy snapped. "You're not going to sell your hair and Lilly's not going to work in a saloon."

"He only wants me to play the piano," Lilly muttered. "The job pays well."

"The piano?" Daisy asked in disbelief.

"Yes," Lilly replied with a sullen tone. "What's wrong with that?"

"What's wrong?" Daisy tried to control her temper. She tapped her chin as if pondering the question. "I suppose the only thing wrong is that you know how to play all of four songs on the piano. Four songs! Mother paid for an entire year of music lessons. After all that, you know *four* songs."

Lilly shrugged as a smile tugged at her lips.

Poppy looked offended. "Four songs isn't so bad. I don't know any."

Daisy set her hand on Poppy's shoulder. "All four songs are *Christmas* carols."

Lilly laughed. "Maybe Mr. Tilson appreciates Christmas carols."

"I think Mr. Tilson appreciates something else," Daisy snapped.

"Like what?" Poppy asked.

Lilly gave a look of wide-eyed innocence. "That's what I want to know."

Daisy shook her head, refusing to play into Lilly's game. It was enough that her sisters had spent the morning making daisy chains out of flowers that weren't actually daisies. That was nothing new. Lilly and Poppy frittered away a great many days. But now Lilly spoke of working in a saloon. A saloon! The idea made her stomach turn.

"Unless..." Lilly sighed.

"Unless what?" Daisy asked.

"Unless Mr. Honeycutt courts you and takes us all in and we move back to wherever he belongs. I heard he's very rich. He has to be if he owns the sawmill."

Daisy closed her eyes and counted backwards from ten. That was her best method of keeping her composure. Lilly laughed softly. Poppy asked if Lilly knew how to play *Away in a Manger*. Lilly said no but promised to learn.

Daisy finished counting. *Five, four, three, two, one.*

She opened her eyes, still feeling plenty irritated with her sisters along with Mr. Honeycutt. She coaxed her lips into a smile. "Thank you for your help."

Poppy laughed. "I found something today."

Daisy ignored Poppy, wishing her sisters would give her a moment's peace so she could get on with supper.

Poppy persisted. "It's a surprise." She continued in a sing-song voice. "Try to guess what it is. I'll give you three chances."

Daisy gave a huff of exasperation. "I'll guess later." She shooed Poppy out of the kitchen, grumbling under her breath.

Lilly laughed softly.

Daisy glanced at Lilly. "Did Poppy happen to find a burlap sack with, say, a hundred dollars?"

Lilly shook her head and sighed. "No, Daisy. I don't think so. I don't know what she found but it's probably nothing. She's talking about selling her hair, so I'm sure she wouldn't have been able to keep finding the money a secret. We all want to find that money."

Daisy sighed as Lilly wandered out of the kitchen. She tried to set her worries aside so she could tend to her chores. She intended to make a nice dinner for Mr. Honeycutt. After all, he was sleeping in the sawmill office so they could remain in the cottage. He would likely change his mind about that arrangement sooner rather than later. In the meantime, she'd try to show her gratitude with a good meal like a roast, vegetables, and a cake for dessert.

Hopefully, he'd like the meal enough that he'd allow them to stay in the cottage for a little longer. Long enough to find Horace's money.

Chapter Fourteen
The Engagement Party

Amelia Honeycutt

Wade McCord gazed at her in a way that Amelia often found aggravating. Standing on the porch, a glass of sweet tea halfway to his lips, he stared, looking slightly dazed with a lopsided smile. He blinked a time or two before composing himself, lifting his glass and taking a swallow of tea.

"I hadn't expected Wade to come," she muttered.

Turning, she narrowed her eyes at the person she blamed for the surprise guest.

Sophie, Amelia's dearest and oldest friend, drew a gasp of surprise. She set her hand on Amelia's arm. "I must apologize. I meant to tell you that my brother would come to lunch. I suppose I forgot."

"You forgot?" Amelia said dryly. "I'm sure his name wasn't on the guest list we discussed because I would have noticed, but he's turned up, after all. Funny how it slipped your mind."

"I had a lot to do," Sophie replied indignantly. "Marie has left me to take care of the engagement details while she sails to Europe."

Sophie had indeed worked hard to arrange an engagement party. It had to be a difficult task when neither the bride nor groom were in attendance. Sophie knew that neither Marie nor Zach would attend, but still insisted on throwing an engagement party. Any excuse to come together for food and fellowship, she declared.

Wade set his glass aside and crossed the porch. "Amelia," he said. "Would you think I'm forward if I said that you look prettier every time that I see you?"

"Wade, you old charmer. I don't think you're forward. But I do think you need to have your eyes checked."

He clasped his hands behind his back. "The color of your gown reminds me of a spring morning."

"Is that so? My dress is purple. What kind of spring morning is purple?"

He took her hand and brushed a kiss across the top. "A perfect spring morning, that's what kind."

"Maybe if a tornado is on its way," Amelia shot back as she tugged her hand from his.

Sophie sighed and laughed softly. "Very pretty words, Wade. Very pretty."

Amelia ignored her friend's obvious matchmaking attempts. She had bigger fish to fry than exchanging pretty words with a notorious ladies' man. When Sophie excused herself, Amelia gestured to the corner of the porch. Wade nodded and escorted her past the other guests.

The McCord home boasted a wrap-around porch. Sunshine brightened the inviting corner, bathing the swing and neighboring chairs with gentle warmth. A profusion of old roses grew in a bed beside the house, lending a subtle perfume to the air.

Wade gestured to the swing. Amelia ignored the suggestion, choosing instead a single chair. Wade might see the empty spot on the swing as an invitation to sit beside her, which would only lead to hard feelings.

"I have a list that I believe will meet with your approval."
He caught her meaning and remained a respectable distance
away, standing by the porch rail.

He no longer regarded her with a spark in his eye. He'd
shifted his demeanor from flirtatious rogue to solemn lawyer.
Amelia felt a wave of gratitude that he wasn't carrying on
about her pretty dress or heaven knows what else. She needed
his legal expertise, not his charm.

"I've almost finished a report for you. I'll send it in a few
days' time. I've come up with a list of five reputable charities
that I believe will meet your approval."

Amelia let out a contented sigh. "Wonderful. Thank you. I
know this isn't the type of work you're accustomed to."

He shook his head. A little of his dashing charm returned
as he smiled at her. "Usually, my clients are trying to safeguard
their money. Not give it away."

"I'm not giving *that* much away. I don't really think of it as
charity. I think of it more as doing my part. I've been blessed
and want to help others, particularly women and children."

For a long moment, Wade didn't reply. He simply looked at
her as if she'd just uttered the most touching words he'd ever
heard. His gaze softened. His head tilted several degrees to the
left.

Amelia narrowed her eyes. "Quit acting daft. Tell me about
the outfits I can send a few dollars to."

Wade drew a deep sigh. "Right. There's a fine children's
home in Fort Worth and another in Abilene. They've both
done a great deal of good. I learned a bit about a teachers'
school in San Marcos along with a nursing school fixing to
open in Galveston."

"Sounds fine," Amelia said. "I like all of those causes. In fact, I've given the nursing school money when it was first proposed. We need more of that sort of thing here in Texas."

Wade smiled.

"What do I owe you?"

"Dinner?"

She waved a dismissive hand and rose from her chair. "Send me a bill, Mr. McCord."

"Yes, ma'am. But don't get mad at me when you see the charge."

"What's that supposed to mean?"

He scoffed. "There's no charge, Amelia. You're my friend. I'll always do anything I can to help you and I'd never, ever send you a bill."

Amelia sighed. "All right. I won't argue. Especially since we're going to be family once my son and your niece get married."

He looked thoughtful. "Maybe so."

Amelia didn't ask what he meant by that comment. Later, when she returned home, she wondered if Wade McCord knew something she didn't.

Chapter Fifteen
Dinner is Shot

Zach

When Zach first met Matt Jonas, the sawmill worker had been tipsy. In truth, the man was beyond tipsy the night before, but he seemed intent on redeeming himself.

The two men spent the rest of the afternoon overseeing the mill. It took a fair bit of work to keep track of the delivery of fresh-cut logs and managing the production of lumber. Dozens of orders awaited fulfillment. Men came looking for work. Equipment needed care. A lumber mill wasn't anything like ranching, Zach had to admit.

Throughout the afternoon, Zach wrestled with the dilemma of supper with the Muldoon girls. The honorable thing to do would be to send word that he couldn't come. Back and forth he argued, silently debating the thorny subject in his mind, trying to figure what was right.

The work in the sawmill kept him busy. Not busy enough to keep his thoughts from sweet Daisy Muldoon. The problem distracted him. In between learning the inner workings of the sawmill and studying the old ledgers, he mulled over what to do. How could he keep his distance from Daisy but still make sure the three sisters were safe and sound?

He felt a deep need to help the girls.

They were vulnerable, stuck here in the middle of a logging town, surrounded by rough types of men. He didn't want to make their troubles worse by accepting an invitation for dinner. If word got out, it might cast them in a bad light.

In the end, he decided to follow his heart. Or perhaps, it was his rumbling stomach he obeyed when he saddled his horse. He stopped along the way to pick some wildflowers, simple white blooms that grew in bunches along the road.

When he arrived, the youngest of the Muldoon sisters skipped down the steps to greet him. Poppy. Was it just yesterday she'd clobbered him with a stout staff? He reached his hand to the lump and found it had diminished somewhat. Fortunately for him, Poppy didn't come with a weapon in hand, just a cheerful smile.

He tied his horse to the hitching post and followed the small girl up the path. He carried the bunch of flowers, noting that they'd already started to droop. He considered pitching them into the tall grass but decided to make the best of things. Perhaps Daisy could revive the blooms if she set them in a cup of water.

"Daisy's been cooking all afternoon." Poppy let out an exasperated huff. "She's been out of sorts, chasing us from the kitchen every chance she got."

"That so?" Zach smiled.

"Lilly talked about you courting my sister."

"What now?"

His thoughts churned with surprise. Not that he didn't want to court Daisy Muldoon. He did. Very much. But that was not an option at this point. He'd just told Daisy he was engaged, although he hadn't had the chance to explain that nature of the engagement. Even if he explained that his engagement would not end with a wedding, he doubted that any sensible woman would want anything to do with him, and from what he could determine so far, Daisy was sensible.

Despite his disappointment about not courting Daisy, he yearned to find a way to help her and his sisters. The problem was everything seemed to be growing more complicated by the moment. Meanwhile, he couldn't help feeling an obligation to Marie. He would need to play his role of fiancé for quite some time, maybe a year or more, until Marie grew tired of Europe and decided to come back home to Texas.

The thing was, a few days ago he didn't really care that he was engaged. In fact, it meant his mother would leave him alone regarding the issue of finding a wife, which was a relief, no doubt. But now that he'd met Daisy, he did care that he was engaged, very much so. The timing of Marie's cockamamie engagement could not have been worse.

Groaning inwardly, he wondered how he'd landed in such a mess.

"Guess what I found today?" Poppy asked, interrupting his thoughts.

Zach tugged her copper braid. "No telling. Buried treasure?"

She glanced back, her eyes sparkling. "Something like that."

"What did you find?"

"You need to guess."

Before Zach could reply, Daisy's younger sister appeared on the path.

"What's your sister's name?" he asked Poppy in a soft voice.

"Lilly."

"Of course. Sorry to say I forgot." Zach knew exactly why her name had slipped his mind. It was because he'd spent so much time thinking of Daisy. Her sisters had faded from his mind. He had to wonder why Lilly regarded him with such a happy and pleased expression.

"Mr. Honeycutt," Lilly said with a wide smile. "My sister has been working her fingers to the bone making tonight's dinner."

Poppy grumbled. "That's not true. She's making a recipe that's easy but dependable. She said it would give her time to work on the floorboards."

"Daisy told me to offer you a glass of tea. She's just finishing getting dressed for dinner," Lilly said cheerfully.

"Sounds mighty nice," Zach said.

The girl darted up to the house as if serving him the glass of tea was a dire emergency.

"Lilly has been fussing all afternoon," Poppy said quietly. "Bossing me and Daisy around. Especially Daisy."

"Why's that?" Zach asked.

The girl scoffed. "Something about looking nice for you when you came to eat dinner. She made Daisy change her dress twice and insisted on helping fix her hair. I think Lilly was trying to make her look pretty for dinner for some reason."

Zach felt his face warm. Despite his discomfort, a smile tugged at his lips. It was hard to imagine Daisy looking anything but pretty. He let out a contented sigh as Poppy prattled on about where she hoped to live one day when she and her sisters left Pineville.

They made their way up the garden path.

Poppy was a little chatterbox. "Daisy says we probably won't have enough money to go back to Biloxi. I told her I want to live in a house where I can have a puppy. That's all I care about. Lilly wants to live someplace bigger than Pineville. A city with sights and sounds. Do you think I'll be able to have a puppy if we live in a different town?"

They reached the cottage steps. Before he could reply, Daisy appeared in the doorway, dressed in a blue gown that accentuated her pretty eyes and narrow frame. Zach couldn't help stare. Distracted by the sight of Daisy Muldoon, he stumbled over an exposed root but managed to regain his footing.

"Mr. Honeycutt," Daisy said shyly. "It's so nice to see you."

He swallowed, trying to dislodge the lump in his throat.

Poppy tugged on his sleeve. "Remember the flowers."

Zach nodded. "Yes. Thank you."

He held out the wilted flowers. Daisy took them, murmuring a few words of thanks.

Poppy went inside, leaving Zach and Daisy alone at the door.

"They looked better a few minutes ago," Zach confessed.

"They're rain lilies," Daisy said. "They're a little delicate. They appear a few days after a rain but vanish just as quickly."

Zach shrugged. "I didn't realize probably because I've never paid too much attention to flowers."

The confession sounded a little ill-mannered. He probably ought to have kept that to himself, especially since all three Muldoon girls were named after flowers.

"They're lovely. Thank you, Mr. Honeycutt." Daisy invited him inside the small cottage.

A savory aroma filled the home, making his stomach rumble. Suddenly, he felt ravenous and looked forward to a good meal. He'd worked hard that day, alternating between paperwork and field work. At one point, he'd returned to the forest with Jonas, strapped clamps to his boots and climbed to the top of a tall pine.

He thought of telling the girls about his adventure when Poppy came to the parlor, carrying a cup of water. She very nearly sloshed the liquid out of the cup. She set the cup down, took the rain lilies and set them in the water.

"Do you know what they're called, Mr. Honeycutt?" she asked.

"Oh, hush, Poppy," Daisy said as she went to the kitchen.

The girl ignored her sister. Sparks of laughter danced in her eyes. She spoke in a hushed tone. Cupping a hand to her mouth, she spoke. "They're called Naked Ladies," she whispered. "Want to know why?"

Zach blinked, unsure how to respond.

"Because they don't have any leaves," Poppy said, bursting into laughter. She pointed to the cup of flowers. "See?"

He leaned closer to inspect the flowers. Sure enough, they didn't have a single leaf. The entire flower consisted of little more than a straight stem and a simple bloom.

"Want to see what I found today?" she asked, as mischief lit a spark in her eye. "Do you?"

Zach figured it would be a short while before dinner was served. Daisy seemed occupied with the meal preparation and Poppy was brimming with excitement. Why not let the girl show off what she'd discovered?

He shrugged. "Sure. You're not going to make me guess?"

"No. I changed my mind. Wait here." The girl skipped away. She appeared a few moments later, carrying a box.

"What do you have there?" Daisy asked, following a step behind.

"None of your beeswax," Poppy replied, setting the box on the dining table. She lifted the lid, set it aside and carefully picked up the small, linen-wrapped bundle. "Uncle Horace always said he'd show me how to shoot his gun."

"You're pretty little to be shooting guns," Zach replied. "Though that tiny thing can't be more than a pea shooter."

"It's not a pea shooter," Poppy replied with clear resentment as she unwrapped the linen.

Daisy drew a sharp breath as she stepped closer. "Poppy, no. Wait!"

"I've waited all day," the girl replied. "I kept trying to show you, but you didn't care. Now I want to show Mr. Honeycutt."

"You shouldn't handle a gun," Daisy snapped. "You're just a child."

Daisy reached over her sister's shoulder and took the weapon. Poppy gave a cry of dismay. Zach held his tongue while the two girls argued. Poppy tried to snatch the gun back. In the midst of the confusion came the report of a gunshot. Not loud like a rifle, more of a pop. Both girls shrieked.

Pain burned a hot trail through his shoulder. He staggered back a step. Gritting his teeth, he gave a deep growl, and clasped his shoulder.

Lifting her hand to her mouth, Daisy grew deathly pale and proclaimed what Zach already knew. "Mr. Honeycutt, you're bleeding."

Chapter Sixteen
A Trip to See Her Youngest Son

Amelia

Amelia awoke in the dark of the moonless night. Drenched in sweat, she sat straight up in bed. "No," she whispered, trying to fend off the fear that gripped her. "It can't be."

After a long moment, her heartbeat slowed. She closed her eyes and did what she always did when she woke in the middle of the night from a terrible dream. She spoke with her late husband.

"George, it's happened again. A nightmare about one of the boys. All along I've fretted about them and that blasted Bethany Brotherhood which was why I asked Zach to go to East Texas, to keep him out of trouble. Why on earth would I dream of him getting shot?"

The wind stirred outside. She waited. Not that George ever answered. Still, she never stopped hoping he might offer a suggestion or two. When she heard nothing more than a solitary cow mooing for her companions, Amelia threw back the blankets and rose from bed.

The only thing that helped after she woke from a bad dream was a cup of hot cocoa. When the boys were small and had nightmares, she always made them cocoa to help chase away their fears. As the years passed and her own bad dreams persisted, Amelia decided she'd use the trusty remedy too.

After she heated the milk and stirred in a generous spoonful of cocoa, and another good helping of sugar, she poured the steaming liquid into a mug and made her way to her study. The house was quiet as the grave. She disliked this time of the night, especially if she was alone. While she loved the new house she'd built a few years before, she didn't like how big and empty it felt whenever she woke in the wee hours of the morning. The eerie silence always troubled her more than she liked to admit.

For the next hour, she worked at her desk, reading reports by the light of her lamp. The activity helped ease her worry somewhat, but she couldn't shake the feeling something was wrong with Zach. While she loved all three boys, she had to admit she had a special bond with her youngest. Over the years, she suspected Zach felt the same strong connection. Perhaps because he'd never known his father since George had died before Zach was born.

She set her papers aside and paced the study, fretting about her sweet-natured boy. She chided herself for sending him clear across the state to tend to some pesky sawmill. Why hadn't she just sold the venture?

As the clock ticked off the minutes and hours, she gave up pacing and worrying. Instead, she lay down on the chesterfield, pulled a blanket over herself and closed her eyes. Bad dreams plagued her for the rest of the night. She awoke as the first rays of sunshine blazed across the study.

To her surprise, the aroma of coffee wafted through the house.

Even more surprising was the appearance of Wade McCord coming into her study with a sheepish look on his face. He carried a cup and saucer and set it down on the table beside the chesterfield. As soon as he'd set it down, he retreated hastily as if concerned she might throw the offering his direction.

Amelia sat up and glared at him to make her disapproval perfectly clear.

"I'm intruding," he said.

"I'll say," she snapped.

"We'd agreed to meet this morning."

She winced, tugging the blanket up. Was that true? Did she have an appointment with Wade? She was still too befuddled by her dreams to know for certain.

"I knocked several times." He sat down in a chair across from her. "When you didn't answer, I took the liberty of letting myself in. You were resting peacefully, so I decided to make coffee."

She let out a soft huff of exasperation and sipped the coffee.

"I'm sorry, Wade. I don't think I can speak with you this morning. I've changed my plans."

His brows lifted. "About giving to a charity?"

"No. Not that. About meeting this morning. I need to go to East Texas to check on Zach."

Wade nodded.

"I had a bad dream. Several in fact."

She waited for him to scoff at her womanish fears. Wade McCord, a bachelor, couldn't imagine what it was like to worry about children. Any minute, he'd ridicule her plans. She didn't care. So what if he thought she was acting foolishly? She didn't need his good opinion, or anyone else's for that matter.

Before he could make some cutting remark, Amelia gave one of her own. "I'm taken aback that you've waltzed right into my home uninvited."

He snorted with amusement. "Waltzed?"

"You ought to consider a lady's reputation. What will folks say if they find out you were in my home without my say-so?"

Wade grinned. "No one would believe it. They'd all expect that if I'd had the gall to try such a reckless endeavor, I'd end up with a limp or blackened eye. Or worse."

Amelia had to admit there was some truth to his words.

Wade leaned forward, resting his elbows on his knees as his expression sobered. "Perhaps you'd agree to me escorting you to Pineville."

She sighed. "Oh, Wade. I'm perfectly capable of making the trip on my own."

"I know," he said. "You're perfectly capable of doing a hundred things on your own. Just the same, I don't care for the notion of you traveling by yourself. Especially across the timber territory. East Texas is rough country. I'd like to come along."

Taking another sip of coffee, she considered the offer. Travel with Wade? What would people say about *that*? Even more than him paying her a visit first thing in the morning, she reckoned. A trip to East Texas would require overnight stays in several towns between Bethany Springs and Pineville. The accommodations would be easy enough to arrange if she were inclined. *If* she were inclined.

She studied his expression and noted the concern in his eyes, the worry he tried to hide. Wade, the old rogue, thought she needed protecting. Did he have any inkling how hard she worked to look formidable? Probably not.

"Maybe," she murmured. "I must admit that you certainly know how to make a good cup of coffee."

Chapter Seventeen
A Nurse in the Making

Daisy

After Daisy shot Mr. Honeycutt in the shoulder, things moved very quickly. He took the gun from her, checked the chambers for other bullets, then set it on top of the mantle. Suddenly, everyone was talking at once, everyone except Mr. Honeycutt who seemed unwilling to let either girl tend to his wound. In fact, Daisy had the distinct impression he intended to doctor himself. He waved off their attempts to help him to a nearby chair.

Daisy watched in horror as the red spot on his shoulder grew in size over the course of the next five minutes while she and Lilly argued about what to do next. Poppy burst into tears and sank to a chair in the corner to cry.

"All I need is a bandage to stop the blood," Zach explained. "I'll get the bullet out somehow."

Somehow.

Daisy cringed at the notion of him caring for his own wound. It was just a shoulder wound, but just the same, it could become infected. Overcome with a crushing sense of guilt, she tried not to think of how close she'd come to causing the man even worse injury or hurting one of her sisters.

She tried to talk herself down.

The man had been shot. Yes. But Daisy tried to tell herself that a shoulder wound couldn't be life-threatening. She offered a quick prayer, thanking God his wound was to the shoulder. Surely that would mean a quick and easy recovery. Surely.

Lilly hurried from the room. A moment later, Daisy heard her rummaging through the hall cabinet. Mr. Honeycutt swayed a little as he glanced down at his wound.

"Mr. Honeycutt, you'll need to remove your shirt," Daisy said, her voice trembling.

His eyes appeared slightly unfocused. "Oh, fine, then. If you insist." He winked at her.

She recoiled. Perhaps the pain was making him delirious. When he tried to unbutton his shirt, he winced at the effort of lifting his injured arm. Daisy ushered him to a nearby chair. This time he went along with her request.

"I'm going to help you take off your shirt."

"All right. I guess you're going to have things your way." He regarded her with bemusement as she undid the top button. "I figure you can call me Zach now."

"Just because I'm helping tend to your injury?"

"Not just that but on account of having shot me in the first place."

Poppy lifted her head and regarded them with a tearful expression. "So, it's Daisy's fault?"

Mr. Honeycutt frowned. "It's no one's fault. It was an accident."

Poppy rubbed her palms across her tear-streaked face. She gave a shuddering sigh and came to his side. "You're very brave, Mr. Honeycutt."

"I'll be all right. Don't you worry, Poppy."

Daisy finished undoing the buttons and helped him out of the shirt. He wore a sleeveless undershirt. Without his shirt gummed against his skin, the blood flowed more freely.

After a fair bit of argument, Daisy and Lilly managed to convince Mr. Honeycutt that he needed to lie down so that they could tend to him. He grumbled and disagreed but was no match for all three Muldoon girls. Grudgingly, he made his way down the hallway. Lilly directed him into the nearest room, the room that belonged to Daisy.

Lilly had found the heavy medical reference book she'd come across the prior evening. She placed it on a nearby table and unpacked the medical bag, setting out linen bandages and various jars of ointment. She hurried from the room, returning a short while later with a steaming basin of water.

After Lilly rolled up her sleeves, she proceeded to care for the wound. First, she washed his arm. Next, she examined the injury. Mr. Honeycutt winced a time or two but other than that, remained still.

Poppy sat on the other side of the bed and patted his arm, murmuring soft words of encouragement.

Daisy sat on the opposite side. She marveled at Lilly's calm skill, and how her younger sister hardly batted an eye as she tended to the wound. Daisy recalled her uncle's words about Lilly, how she was a heap smarter than most folks thought. He liked to talk about how one day the middle Muldoon sister would surprise them all.

Daisy hadn't quite believed Uncle Horace. Lilly spent more time tending to her wild, unruly locks than she did to anything of importance. And yet, the same empty-headed girl had stepped up to manage this emergency. She worked efficiently and without a single sign of distress. For her part, Daisy could hardly stand to look at Mr. Honeycutt's shoulder, much less try to clean the wound.

Lilly paged through Uncle Horace's medical book, talking under her breath. "Let's see. Dental Abnormalities. Vascular

Concerns. Ah! Here we are, Extractions of Bullets and Foreign Debris."

Daisy cringed and rubbed her brow. She'd been such a fool. Her intention had been to take the gun from Poppy, but in trying to do so, she'd accidentally shot a person. Her stomach clenched with a wave of nausea. The wound was superficial but that hardly mattered, not when it meant a man had a lead ball in his arm.

Lilly washed the tools in a solution she'd found in the bag, then rinsed them in the steaming water.

Mr. Honeycutt eyed her as she worked and grimaced. "I reckon this is going to happen, even though I'm sure we can wait a spell. Sometimes bullets work their way out."

Daisy swallowed, trying to dislodge the lump in her throat. "If we don't get the ball out of your arm, the wound will fester. And we don't have a doctor anywhere in a hundred miles."

He nodded and closed his eyes. "Alrighty. Looks like your sister knows what she's doing."

Poppy knit her brow. Daisy knew she was about to explain that Lilly knew next to nothing. Daisy shot her a warning look, effectively shushing the girl.

Lilly worked quietly and steadily. When Daisy eyed the surgical instruments, she felt sick to her stomach.

Not Lilly. Her sister wasn't the least bit squeamish. Daisy watched her sister work, amazed at her calm demeanor. Lilly's hands were steady as she selected a pair of pincers. She snapped them a time or two. Poppy gave a small whimper and squeezed her eyes shut.

Daisy took Mr. Honeycutt's hand in hers. "I'm so very sorry," she said quietly.

He smiled. "It's all right. It could have been a great deal worse."

He nodded in the direction of Poppy who still had her eyes squeezed shut. Daisy's stomach somersaulted as she once more considered the full implication of his words. It had been an accident, that was true, but one of them could have been severely injured or worse. It could have easily been Poppy since she'd been the one to find the gun.

Mr. Honeycutt squeezed her hand to soothe her fear. He gave her a cheerful smile. "I've been through worse than this."

Poppy gasped. "You have? What's worse than getting shot?"

"I broke my arm on a cattle drive. I had to ride three hundred miles with a busted arm. Another time, I dislocated my shoulder and had to fix it myself which can be a little tricky. Then there was the time when I accidentally-"

Daisy shook her head. "Please, don't tell us anymore."

Lilly worked diligently. Every so often, she'd mutter a word of encouragement. In the silence of the room, she explained that she saw the bullet and was convinced she could extract it. Poppy looked faint. Mr. Honeycutt appeared stoic, as if he hardly noticed any pain. Daisy just wanted Lilly to be done as quickly as possible.

After what felt like an eternity, Lilly drew a sharp breath. Mr. Honeycutt winced. With a radiant smile, Lilly held up the pincers to show them the bullet. Daisy stared in disbelief. Lilly, her sweet sister, had just taken a bullet from a man's arm, a bullet that Daisy had fired from Uncle Horace's lost gun.

Everyone spoke at once. Mr. Honeycutt murmured his thanks. Lilly explained that she was only happy to help. Daisy praised her sister's steady nerves. Poppy mumbled a few words before crumpling onto the bed beside Mr. Honeycutt and dissolving into tears once more.

He gave Poppy a sympathetic glance, patted her shoulder with his uninjured arm then turned his attention to Daisy with a sheepish smile. "I'm just glad I didn't pass out in front of the three charming Muldoon ladies."

Chapter Eighteen
Zach Decides to Stay

Zach

The aroma of Daisy's cooking made his mouth water, and despite the ache in his shoulder, he was ready to eat. He was ravenous. The aroma of Daisy's cooking filled the cottage with sumptuous smells he remembered from his childhood, huge dinners on special days like Easter and Christmas.

While he appreciated the fine dinner, he didn't particularly like how much Daisy fussed over him. It was as if he'd suddenly turned into an invalid.

She stayed close to his side, attended to his every need like he was a child. Before they came to the table, she directed him to wear her uncle's shirt so that he wouldn't catch a chill. He wondered where that notion came from considering it was a fine spring evening.

Next, she asked, no, *demanded*, that he sit at the head of the table because the sturdy chair would be easier for him. Something about the armrests or maybe the padded back support. It all felt a tad awkward, and not just because her uncle's sleeves were far too short and made him feel like he wore a shirt he'd outgrown.

No, Zach wasn't used to a young woman's attention. She hovered over him, serving him a generous portion of beef, roast potatoes, and creamed greens. He figured she might stop there, but no such luck. Next thing he knew, Daisy was cutting up his meat.

Lilly and Poppy sat, watching. Both of them tried not to smile at their sister's mother-henning.

He sighed as she cut his roast. He might as well give in to her attention since she wasn't going to let up. Besides, he sort of liked having her so close. In truth, he liked it a lot. The girl was powerfully distracting. A hint of her floral soap wafted over him. He stole a quick look at the soft and delicate skin along the curve of her shoulder. Daisy was lovely. Her feminine features made him forget his thoughts.

He vaguely considered telling her not to fret over him so much. Then again, maybe he wouldn't stop her. Not just yet. Daisy's attention wasn't half bad. In fact, he might just gripe a little more about his injury. Especially if his complaining would earn him an extra helping of Daisy's doting.

She took a seat beside him and asked him to say a blessing over the meal. He obliged, pleased that she'd asked. He glanced around the table. Lilly, who seemed to be playing the part of matchmaker, regarded him with an amused smile. Poppy, sitting to his side, tucked her hand in his and waited for his prayer. Daisy sat on his other side. He started to reach for Daisy's hand but winced as he tried to lift his arm. She quickly reached over and gripped his hand under the table, to save him from any more pain. He said a quick blessing, the same he'd heard so often growing up.

"Give us grateful hearts, Father, for all thy mercies, and make us mindful of the needs of others. Through Jesus Christ our Lord. Amen."

The girls, heads bowed, murmured a soft "Amen."

Daisy was the first to speak, directing them to serve themselves. The girls began passing plates around as they spoke of various subjects. The goings-on in town. How the mercantile had a paltry supply of fabric and buttons.

Zach ate his dinner with relish. As he enjoyed the meal, Daisy continued her attention to his every need. Somehow, ever since she'd shot him a few hours earlier, her voice sounded softer, gentler, and especially caring. Wounding a fellow seemed to change a woman's demeanor, he noted with amusement.

Instead of trying to keep her distance from him, Daisy spoke warmly and with deep concern. Especially whenever he winced or rubbed his bandage. Which he managed to do with some regularity for the duration of the meal.

When the dinner came to a close, he chided himself for taking advantage of the situation. It was time to go, he decided. He couldn't linger and enjoy the company of Daisy Muldoon. Sure, he wanted to remain in the cottage, but he also wanted to safeguard the girl's reputation.

Pineville was a small town with scarcely any womenfolk. For that reason, a girl's reputation was especially precious. The men might indulge in all sorts of vices, but a woman couldn't risk the merest whisper of scandal. Not in a logging town.

The sun's last rays softened and faded. Dusk turned to twilight. The shadows lengthened and dimmed as the first evening stars twinkled in the purple sky. Even though he didn't really want to leave, he knew it was time. He thanked Daisy and her sisters for the meal, pushed back from the table and got to his feet.

"I ought to be on my way," he said.

"You're leaving?" Lilly asked. She scowled and shook her head. "I should change the dressing on your wound."

She gestured to the medical volume on a nearby table. "My uncle's book says it's very important."

The girl had pored over the pages, jotting notes, and talking to herself about wet and dry dressings while Daisy served dinner. He could tell she intended to see the treatment through.

"You shouldn't leave," Daisy followed. "It wouldn't be prudent."

"I'm making a linseed plaster," Lilly said. "It's warming on the stove."

Zach winced. "A linseed plaster?"

Lilly knit her brow. "That's right."

He chuckled. "Sounds tempting. I've *always* wanted a warm linseed plaster. What could be better?" The elder Muldoon girls regarded him with solemn expressions. Neither girl so much as smiled at his joke. Sobering, he spoke, "See, I'm fine. I don't need a wound dressing."

Silence followed.

He shook his head. "Linseed? I'm pretty sure that's what we feed our cattle."

Lilly bristled. "A linseed dressing is an excellent wound dressing. According to my uncle's medical book, more men succumb to infection than the gunshot itself. I need to dress the wound before you retire this evening, and I need to do it again first thing in the morning. You ought to stay here."

Zach scoffed. "I'm bunking at the mill. Not that I want to sleep in a narrow, too-short cot, but I can't stay in this cottage. Not until you girls are ready to leave Pineville."

"You should sleep here," Lilly said. "It's simple."

Daisy gave a breathless laugh. "Here?"

Lilly narrowed her eyes. "Don't you want Mr. Honeycutt to recover?"

"Of course. Yes. Goodness." Daisy looked pale.

"He can sleep in the back room," Lilly explained. "That way, he'd be away from the rest of the house but close enough if he needs help or tending."

Zach didn't give too much thought to his injury. He'd played up the pain and severity during dinner, but he didn't really worry about the wound. He and his brothers had grown up working hard, getting hurt all the time. Dozens of times. As a cowboy, he'd suffered loads of deep cuts, sprains, and broken bones. Injuries were all a fact of life, as far as he was concerned.

His latest wound didn't trouble him much. The bullet was out. The injury would heal, given time.

What troubled him more was Daisy Muldoon. The girl upset his usual equanimity. He could see how much his injury troubled her. He knew, too, how troubles weighed upon her shoulders, especially since her uncle had passed.

He wished there was some way to ease her worries.

Ignoring Lilly's dire predictions, he got ready to leave the cottage. He thanked the Muldoons for their hospitality and took his leave. Daisy followed him from the house and down the path to where his horse waited in the corral.

"Perhaps you should stay," she said as he checked his cinch.

"I can't stay here," he said as he adjusted the bridle chinstrap.

He turned to face her. The sight of her, standing just a pace away, stole his breath.

A honey-colored lock fell across her brow. He wanted to brush it aside. No. He wanted something more. He yearned to gather Daisy up, along with her sisters and take them away from Pineville. She didn't belong in this rough-hewn logging town. If only he could find a way to help her without offending her pride.

If only...

He resolved to seek some sort of remedy. He'd make sure that once Daisy and her sisters left Pineville, they would be well situated. If he wrote his mother and laid out the problem, she'd probably offer some plan. Mama prided herself on fixing problems even more than she prided herself on making money. He'd write her a letter that very evening, leaving out any mention of getting shot. No, he didn't need to bother his mother with that sort of pesky detail.

"Can I at least take a look at your wound?" Daisy asked.

He heaved a deep sigh. Even his mother didn't fret this much over him and his brothers. He had to admit her fretting wasn't half bad. "All right."

He unbuttoned his shirt and tugged it back. He was sure the small wound was perfectly fine but wanted to convince Daisy.

"Oh, dear," she said.

Zach glanced down. To his surprise, the wound looked red and angry. He shook his head and buttoned up his shirt. "Daisy," he said gently. "I'm fine. The bullet was small, and it just barely glanced the side of my arm."

She nodded then lifted her gaze to meet his. "Uncle Horace didn't think his injury was going to cause him much trouble. Nor did anyone else. When the logging crew brought him to the house, carrying him on a gurney, his men promised he'd be fine in a day or so. But he wasn't fine."

"Daisy," he murmured. "Sweetheart..."

His words faded off as he tried to find a fitting response. He wanted to explain that he'd be perfectly fine. That she fretted for no reason. At the same time, he didn't want to brush off her worry.

Behind her words lay a great deal of pain and loss. The girls had lost a warm, kind family member. When their uncle passed, the three young girls were left alone in the rough, uncivilized world of a logging camp.

"I've already imposed on you, Mr. Honeycutt," Daisy said. "I can't bear to think of you sleeping in that dusty sawmill with your injured arm."

With a deep sigh, he relented. "I suppose I could leave before sunrise, so no one notices I've been a guest in your home."

She smiled with relief. "Having you stay overnight is untoward to be sure, but just the same, I do like the notion of you nearby. Lilly's quite intent on furthering her nursing skills."

"If it would make you feel better." He lifted his hand to brush the stray lock of hair from her eyes. When a soft rose blush warmed her cheeks, he felt his breath catch in his throat. "In fact, it sounds mighty fine, Miss Muldoon."

She smiled and nodded.

"I can sleep on the porch."

"No. Of course not. You can stay in the back room. We can keep it a secret."

Zach spoke softly. "I won't say a word, if you don't."

Her blush deepened. "No. Of course, I won't tell anyone."

Chapter Nineteen
Breakfast After the Shooting

Daisy

As much as she fretted about having Zach Honeycutt stay in her home, Daisy felt a tremendous sense of relief. The shock of injuring him made her sick. The only thing worse was the possibility of him getting an infection or suffering somehow from the wound.

She woke several times in the night, tiptoed to his room to make sure he was well. She carried a lamp which cast a golden glow across the room and over Mr. Honeycutt's face as he slept. The soft light illuminated his handsome features. Watching a man, a near-stranger, as he slept was the most unseemly thing she'd ever done.

And yet...

She allowed herself to linger and admire his strong profile, broad shoulders, and noble bearing. Her thoughts wandered to romantic notions, the way his hand felt wrapped around hers, the way he smiled at her or the way he showed her sisters such consideration and kindness.

And then she recalled with a stark sense of cold shock, the man she admired was betrothed, engaged to a young lady. She had no business thinking any such girlish thoughts about a man who belonged to another.

Overcome with guilt and sadness, she hurriedly withdrew and returned to her own room.

The next morning, she rose before dawn to prepare breakfast. She brewed a pot of coffee, fried bacon and scrambled a dozen eggs. Mr. Honeycutt wandered into the kitchen with a smile, looking a little sleepy but ready to take on the day. She gave him a cup of coffee.

"How's your shoulder?" she asked, trying to sound businesslike.

He flexed his arm. "You know, I think it's doing even better than before you shot me."

She winced. "Mr. Honeycutt, please."

"I'm just joshing." He took a swallow of his coffee. "Quit fretting. I'm fine."

She finished cooking breakfast and served him a generous portion of eggs and bacon. After he gave thanks for the meal, he began to eat, complimenting her on the fine breakfast.

They sat at the table in the quiet of the morning, talking about family. She spoke of Uncle Horace and his kindly ways. He hadn't ever intended to be a family man, but he'd taken Daisy and her two sisters in without a word of complaint. If anything, Daisy explained, Uncle Horace relished having the three of them under his roof.

"He used to tell people that the three of us were 'his girls' and that when we came, we changed his house into a home. He could be a little bit of a curmudgeon at times, a little set in his ways, but he always made us feel cherished. It seemed we were just getting to know each other when he passed away," Daisy said sadly. "At times, I think it's been hardest on Poppy."

"You too," Mr. Honeycutt said thoughtfully. "You've had to keep it all going. All on your own."

She smiled. "The good Lord has provided for us. I just need to keep up my faith that He will continue to provide and that we need to accept His plan for us."

"That's right," he replied. "Simple but not easy."

Mr. Honeycutt left just as the sun peeked over the horizon. She stood on the steps in the first rays of dawn, watching as he rode down the road and disappeared past the stand of pine trees. The morning breeze stirred, here and there, rustling through the pine boughs. She tugged her shawl closer and kept her gaze fixed on the spot on the road where he'd ridden just a moment before.

For some reason, she felt a small pang of loneliness. As much as she resisted the notion, she had to admit that she liked having him nearby. Even though she'd spent a restless night, trying not to think of Mr. Honeycutt, she felt comforted in the knowledge that he was there in the cottage.

"He belongs to another," she whispered in the early morning quiet.

Chapter Twenty
Back at Work

Zach

In the beginning, when his mother first mentioned the East Texas sawmill, Zach figured it would be an easy way to help his family. In particular, it would help his mother. Lord knew she worked hard. She toiled long days from even before he could recall, seeing as she was widowed so young. After his father passed in the war, Mama needed to not only keep food on the table but raise up three boys in her spare time.

Those were lean years, she liked to say.

It always pained him to hear about the lean years. He liked to think he could put his shoulder to the wheel, take on a good share of work and give her a little reprieve from her never-ending tasks. When he heard she'd acquired a sawmill, he decided right then he'd take that burden from his mother. He'd run the venture till she could turn around and sell it.

After all, how hard could it be to run a sawmill?

That's what he told himself all the way out to Pineville.

Turns out, the answer was a little different then he imagined.

In fact, running a sawmill was plenty hard.

And that was before he took a bullet to the shoulder. His shoulder didn't bother him too much, but it still took some effort to manage things with a sore arm. The big saw, the one that sat right in the middle of the mill, seemed to require more babying than an orphaned calf. The saw was powered by various belts that liked to loosen and fly off their track.

Several times a day, the entire operation of cutting lumber ground to a halt. The only way to fix the belt, turns out, was for someone to climb over the machinery and wrangle the belt back onto the big, steel wheel that propelled it. It was a tricky job, one that required a fair bit of strength, which was how Zach ended up taking care of matters.

Few of the workers could manage the job properly.

The belt came loose early in the morning, and again before lunch. The third time Zach clambered across the span of machinery, he was ready to cuss the old saw. And the rest of the mill too.

As he worked to fix the darned belt, he resisted the urge to complain about the saw or sawmills in general. Mostly on account of Daisy. If he hadn't come to Pineville, he never would have met Daisy. His shoulder ached, and sweat trickled down his neck, but the thought of Daisy made him too happy to grumble.

He considered each of her qualities as he climbed up the ladder.

First, he appreciated the way her lips curved to a sweet smile. She was often a little reluctant about smiling. A little shy. But then the smile won over her reluctance and lit her whole face.

Next was the scent of her fair skin. Sort of like honey mixed with flowers, he decided.

Finally, there was the sweet, joyful sound of her laughter. It didn't come easy. No, Daisy guarded her laughter even more than her smiles, but when she gave in to her laughter, well, Daisy Muldoon certainly made him happy he'd come to Pineville.

It wasn't easy, but he needed to push thoughts of Daisy Muldoon to the back of his mind. The saw needed his attention now. He swung from the frame and climbed to reach the loose belt. Meanwhile, the giant circular saw sat a few feet away, idle yet strangely menacing. He grimaced. The jagged blade wouldn't spin till he fixed the belt, but the pointed teeth still seemed plenty fierce.

Sawmills were different territory. He decided that right about the same time he finished tending to the loose belt. Turning away, he felt a wash of gratitude that he was a cowboy through and through. He'd rather take on an ornery bull than some cantankerous sawblade.

Throughout the afternoon, a slow steady rain fell. The rain never amounted to more than a continuous drizzle, but quickly rendered the roads near impassable. The oxcarts sank to their axles. The oxen strained with their loads and the drivers, concerned for their animals, told Zach they couldn't continue without risking injury.

The loggers quit early as well. One by one, the saws ground to a stop and the mill grew quiet except for the sound of rainfall. Zach would have liked to leave early too but was delayed. One team of loggers quarreled with another, accusing them of venturing into their territory. The men crowded in his office, growing more belligerent. Zach agreed to hike out to the forest to settle the dispute.

The gray afternoon slipped into a murky dusk. By the time Zach settled the argument and headed to the cottage, it was late. The girls would have eaten supper without him, or he certainly hoped so. When he reached their home, his heart leapt to see the lamplight glowing from the windows.

He unsaddled his horse in the shed. With the a few handfuls of dry hay, he rubbed the horse down. The animal had to be cold and miserable too. He left the gelding in his stall with more hay and a bucket of oats. Trudging along the slick trail, he neared the house and spied a figure in the doorway. In an instant, he recognized the slim form as belonging to Daisy.

"I'm sorry to keep you waiting," he said, removing his cowboy hat. He tipped it over to drain the water that had accumulated.

In the flickering lamplight, he noted the worry around her eyes. "Everything's all right, Mr. Honeycutt?"

"It's fine. Just delayed is all."

"Thank goodness. I fretted, worried there might have been an accident. It seems not a week goes by without some calamity."

He knew that to be true. Sawmills were dangerous territory. The men at the mill and those in the forest all spoke of mashed fingers, broken bones and other grave injuries. Zach had to admit that the lumber business wasn't kind to the workers. His thoughts drifted to one of the bigger saws, an enormous blade driven by a Corliss steam engine, gunning with the force of several hundred horsepower.

He winced. There hadn't been any calamities. Not today.

"No, ma'am." He smiled. "Not a single calamity."

"I kept dinner in the oven. I set out some of my uncle's things. You'd best get out of your wet clothes and come sit by the fire." She flushed with a sudden awkwardness. "Please."

He nodded, left his sodden boots on the porch, and did as she'd asked. Horace's shirt was a little tight. The pants were a tad short, but at least they were dry. He hung his wet things over a rail, so he'd have dry clothes come morning.

A short while later, he sat comfortably by the warm blaze enjoying a fine dish of chicken and dumplings. In the stillness of the evening, Daisy sat nearby, talking quietly about her day as he devoured the meal.

A quick glance at the clock on the mantle told him it was later than he suspected. Half-past ten. No wonder the house was quiet.

"I've kept you up," he said apologetically.

"It's no trouble. Lilly was tired after spending half the day reading that medical volume. I declare, she's hardly taken her nose from that book. Every so often, she tells me about a tropical illness or childhood ailment. She's worn out, probably from reading about so many frightful diseases. She's gone to bed for the night, but she gave me explicit instructions about your bandage and dressing. I have some linseed dressing on the stove."

He shrugged. "I'd rather have a second helping of supper."

She smiled and took his plate, returning a moment later with seconds.

This time he ate more slowly, taking time to converse with Daisy. Sitting by the crackling blaze, enjoying the warmth, the food and the gentle companionship, he felt secretly pleased that Lilly and Poppy were already asleep.

Daisy spoke of her life before coming to Pineville, living with her mother and father on the fine estate of a Biloxi shipbuilder. She avoided delving too deeply into sad subjects such as her parents' death. On that matter, she simply spoke of their mercifully quick passing. Most of the talk concerned life in Biloxi.

"Every so often, Mother and Father would take us out on a sea excursion." Her eyes shone. "My mother and I especially loved the water. Lilly thought it was dull and Poppy often got sea-sick."

"I've never ventured out on a ship," Zach said. "Not sure if I'd like it. I have to say I prefer fields of green and big open sky. I prefer ranch land to the forests around Pinewood."

"You intend to return soon to Bethany Springs?"

"Maybe. I know a couple of outfits would like to buy the sawmill. I'm only here to help out my mother. I'm better suited to life in the saddle than running a big, noisy mill."

"We had sawmills in Biloxi too. Uncle Horace always wanted to come to Texas though." She sighed.

"Some men have that urge to travel and see the sights. Me, I'm too fond of my family. I like to see my ornery brothers every so often. And I'm always happy to see my mother." He winked. "Especially since I'm her favorite."

She laughed softly and took his plate to the kitchen. Hoping she might stay a little longer, he added wood to the fire. As he stirred the coals, sparks hissed and shot up the chimney. Flames burst from the glowing bed of coals and soon the fire burned merrily once more.

After the long day in the mill and after dealing with obstinate machines and men, he was grateful to sit by the fire with Daisy. The deep chill slowly ebbed from his bones. He yearned to linger and was pleased when she returned and took her seat with no sign of weariness.

When it grew too late for conversation, Zach banked the coals and bid her good night. She wished him a good night as well and left him in the parlor, vanishing down the darkened hallway. Shortly after, he made his way to bed. Lying awake in the darkness, he listened to the relentless rain. He turned his thoughts to evening prayers and gave thanks for the time he shared with Daisy by the fireside.

He spent a restless night in the company of strange dreams. Vivid imaginings of peculiar trees, growing in an odd land that was neither Bethany Springs nor Pineville. Each movement he made sent a stab of pain through his shoulder. Distantly, he heard the soft feminine and familiar voices. The final recollection before he drifted into a deep slumber was the soothing touch of a cool palm upon his fevered brow.

Chapter Twenty-One
A Turn for the Worse

Daisy

When Mr. Honeycutt didn't awaken in the predawn dark, Daisy let him sleep. It had rained all night and, as she lit the stove, thunder unfurled overhead. The blast shook the timbers of the cottage. Even the most foolhardy of loggers wouldn't venture into the forest when thunderstorms rolled over Pineville. Surely, Mr. Honeycutt could enjoy an extra hour of rest.

She heated a pan, added some fat, and when it was melted, tossed in a diced onion. It sizzled. The savory aroma wafted across the kitchen as Daisy cut slices of bacon.

Lilly wandered into the kitchen, yawning, dressed but with her lovely copper locks unbound. Daisy noted her sister's pretty hair with a pang of envy. She was certain, if given the chance, Mr. Honeycutt, like countless other men in Pineville, would steal glances at Lilly.

An ache tugged at her heart. She chided herself for her foolish yearnings. Mr. Honeycutt was engaged to another young lady, a girl who likely came from a wealthy family. Why should she, a penniless orphan, care about Mr. Honeycutt? If he wanted to admire Lilly, he ought to do just as he pleased.

She pushed the base thoughts aside. It was time for breakfast. Not for petty sibling rivalry.

"Goodness, Daisy." Lilly peered at the pan on the counter. "You didn't use much of the linseed. Or any of it from the looks of things."

"Hm?" Daisy frowned. "Linseed?"

As soon as she asked, a knot of dread formed deep in her chest.

Lilly held up the pot that held the poultice, the same poultice Daisy was supposed to apply to the wound, the same wound Mr. Honeycutt suffered when she'd accidentally shot him. *That* linseed.

"Oh." Daisy's heart fell. She stared at the pot. No. It couldn't be. It was impossible she'd forgotten the simple assignment. And yet she had. She'd spent the evening chatting with Mr. Honeycutt, another woman's betrothed, all while forgetting one simple but very necessary task.

"Oh?" Lilly asked. "What does that mean?"

Daisy wiped her damp palms down her apron.

"I don't know... exactly... what came over me," Daisy said slowly. And then she began to speak all at once, a rush of words. They came quickly, starting with Mr. Honeycutt arriving late from the sawmill, dripping wet, changing from his soggy, muddy clothes, eating dinner, the two of them sitting by the fire and talking at length.

Lilly nodded, speechless, still holding the evidence of Daisy's neglect.

"We talked for some time. You see." Daisy gestured, her hands waving before her as she searched for words. "Not too long. Perhaps till midnight or so."

To her surprise, Lilly's lips curved into a smile. "Midnight?"

"It might have been before midnight. Who can say about these sorts of things?"

Lilly's eyes sparkled as she whispered, "Did he kiss you?"

"Of course, he did *not!*" Daisy gave her sister a stern look. Lilly didn't know about Mr. Honeycutt's engagement, but, nonetheless, her question was unseemly. It was wrong. Lilly probably asked because of the various times she'd let a handsome, charming young man steal a kiss from her. Or so Daisy suspected.

"It seems he's sleeping late." Lilly spoke in a tone that was more matter-of-fact than teasing.

Daisy nodded. "I suppose he might be oversleeping. A tad."

Lilly set the linseed poultice on a nearby table. With a potholder, she shoved the iron pan with the bacon off the heat and urged Daisy out of the kitchen. "Let's check in on him, shall we? I don't dare send you by yourself, you little flirt. You're likely to kiss my poor patient."

Shock swept over Daisy. She reddened. "Would you hush already?"

Lilly snickered with deep amusement.

When they reached Mr. Honeycutt's door, Lilly shoved her in front. Daisy nearly tripped but recovered in time to save herself a fall at the doorstep. She lifted her hand and knocked lightly. "Mr. Honeycutt?"

A rumbling sound greeted her ear. Mr. Honeycutt's deep baritone cut through the silence. "Daisy Muldoon."

Lilly gave a soft, surprised laugh.

Daisy elbowed her. "Are you well, sir?"

"Sir..." Lilly snorted. "*Sir*? Truly? And you're still calling him Mr. Honeycutt? I'm sure you can call a man by his given name once you've shot him in the shoulder."

Daisy ignored her. "You've overslept. Can I bring you breakfast? Some coffee?"

"So many trees," he muttered.

Daisy shook her head, not understanding his words.

"Not sure about all the... trees." His words drifted off.

Lilly drew a sharp breath. A moment before, she'd been grinning and teasing. Now she looked somber, her expression taut with worry. "He's running a fever."

Daisy stood rooted to the floor, filled with self-reproach. Guilt fell over her like a heavy shroud. First, she'd injured the poor man, who'd been nothing but kind to her and her sisters. Next, she'd neglected to care for his wound.

And now he suffered from an infection and risked all manner of fearful outcomes.

Daisy swallowed, trying to dislodge the lump in her throat. Lilly looked pale and stricken. For a moment, their eyes locked, but in the next instant, Lilly pushed past, bursting into Mr. Honeycutt's room. Daisy started to follow, but Lilly stopped her and sent her back to the kitchen.

Chapter Twenty-Two
A Day to Rest

Zach

The day dawned gray and drizzly. He lay in bed, wondering where he was, a slow realization coming over him when one of the Muldoon girls hurried into the room with a basin of water. It was the middle one. She glanced his way, a frown etched on her features.

"Where's Daisy?" he asked, his voice rough from a restless night.

"She's making you some broth."

His stomach turned. He shifted under the blankets, grimacing when a pain shot up his arm. Muttering under his breath, he closed his eyes, hoping to fall back asleep and wake feeling a little better. His mind wouldn't let him rest. Instead, he imagined Daisy working at the stove, trying to help him heal from whatever peculiar ailment troubled him that morning.

"I overslept," he muttered. He sighed wearily, trying to recall the middle girl's name. His scattered thoughts darted here and there but the name didn't come to him. Rain drummed down on the roof, blurring his mind. Time passed. How much, he couldn't say. Finally, he gave in and asked.

"What's your name?"

"Poppy."

The voice came from right next to the bed. He opened his eyes with surprise to find that the youngest Muldoon girl stood beside the bed, not the middle girl. She held a porcelain doll in her small hands, and quietly offered it to him. He shook his head, trying to clear his thoughts. What a strange night it had been.

When he didn't immediately accept the toy, Poppy lifted the blankets and tucked the doll next to him. She smoothed the covers, gave him a knowing look as she nodded solemnly. Softly, she whispered, "Mrs. Cavendish will make everything better."

"Much obliged," Zach murmured.

The girl smiled.

"What's your sister's name?" he asked quietly.

Poppy cupped a hand to her mouth and whispered, "Lilly."

Not a moment later, Lilly came to the bedside, setting a tray on a nearby table. She glanced at the doll but gave no sign of having seen the toy tucked next to him. Instead, she began tending to his wounded shoulder, wringing out a linen cloth.

"If you roll over, I can tug the shirt down," she said, her tone stern.

He did as she asked, not daring to argue. Lilly pulled the shirt back and muttered under her breath, words that suggested she was displeased with the sight of his wound. Just as his thoughts wandered back to Daisy, she appeared at his bedside. Quietly, she took a nearby chair and offered a soft smile.

"Daisy," he said. "You're like a ray of sunshine on this rainy morning."

"It's my fault that you're sick, Mr. Honeycutt."

Her voice trembled. She clasped her hands on her lap and blinked as if trying to hold back tears. Despite the pain in his arm, he reached to take her hands in his.

"Please stay still, Mr. Honeycutt." Lilly's voice was sharp and uncompromising.

He sighed. "Why is it your fault, sweetheart? It was just an accident."

"I was supposed to dress your wound last night."

"Don't fret." He closed his eyes. "I'm sure I'll be better soon, sunshine."

Daisy and Lilly looked at each other for a moment before Lilly returned to her task. Lilly dabbed his wound with the linen cloth. He shifted to a more comfortable position.

"Hold still," she demanded.

Despite the circumstances, Zach felt his lips curve into a smile. He opened one eye to find Daisy watching him intently. His smile widened.

"Your sister sorta scares me," he said. "She's meaner than she looks."

From the other side of the bed, he heard Lilly's surprised laugh.

Daisy's lips tugged into a faint smile. "Mean? Yes. You have no idea."

Lilly huffed as she gently dried the wound. "Aren't you supposed to be making broth for Mr. Honeycutt?"

"Don't go, Daisy," Zach said. "Stay a little longer."

For a long moment, no one spoke. Lilly applied the poultice. The linseed stung at first but then felt comforting. Silence filled the room as his mind wandered with fevered thoughts. He shivered beneath the blanket.

"I'll be done soon," Lilly said. "Then we'll get you under the covers."

"Along with Mrs. Cavendish," Daisy said with a quiet but playful tone.

"Did you know there's a nursing school that just opened in Galveston?" he mused.

Neither girl responded.

Zach went on, growing weary as he waited for Lilly to finish. "You'd be a fine nurse, Lilly. You ought to study there. It's a year or two. Not sure. Mama might know more."

Daisy looked at her hands folded in her lap, pursing her lips with dismay. Lilly kept on with her task but remained silent too.

"Did I say something wrong?" he asked.

Daisy lifted her gaze but didn't answer.

Lilly spoke before her sister could reply. Her tone was light and conversational, as if talking about nothing more than the inclement weather. "Maybe one day," she said airily. "Maybe when the Muldoon family's ship comes in."

"Doubt your ship is coming to the piney woods." Zach chuckled. "My mother can help out, Lilly. She gives the school heaps of money."

He sensed the girls' unease. Something about his remark troubled them, but what it was, he couldn't fathom. His thoughts and concerns about the girls drifted off as weariness washed over him.

Closing his eyes, he sank deeper into the soft bed as Lilly secured his bandage. A moment later, he heard her footsteps echo down the hallway. He sensed Daisy draw near as she gently tucked the blankets around him. Her scent wafted around him, teased his senses, and lingered as he fell back to a deep sleep.

Chapter Twenty-Three
An Unplanned Stay in Austin

Amelia

Near the end of their first day of travel, Amelia and Wade encountered a small fly in the ointment. It brought their progress to a standstill. Amelia's trusty gelding threw a shoe just outside of Austin. She'd noticed when her horse began to favor one leg.

Thankfully, Wade found the lost shoe when he backtracked a quarter mile or so. Even though they had the missing shoe, it hadn't done them much good. The farrier couldn't shoe the horse till late that evening which meant they'd need to stay over in Austin.

"We can stay in Sophie and Robert's rooms at the Driskill," Wade offered as they stood in the doorway of the livery barn.

"We?" Amelia asked, raising her brow. She wanted to be clear that their time together would not only *appear* respectable, but it would also *be* respectable. No *appearance* of tomfoolery. No tomfoolery.

The prior night, they'd taken rooms at separate inns. Now Wade was talking about staying in the same locale?

"I will stay in my own room," Wade hastened to add.

"I suppose we don't have much of a choice."

Wade gave the livery hands instructions about bedding down the horses, the feed the animals would require and when he and Mrs. Honeycutt would return in the morning. He added some directions about the mule's baggage, directing the men to deliver it to the Driskill.

Without another word, he tucked her hand in the crook of his arm and did his darnedest to act the charming host as they walked the short distance to the hotel. The town of Austin bustled around them. It seemed it had doubled in size since the last time she visited. New shops and businesses had sprung up. People crowded the walkways. Wagons, buggies, and cowboys on horseback filled the streets.

The noise jarred her senses. She wasn't used to the big town and felt a slight sense of overwhelm. Wade, on the other hand, seemed energized by the hustle. He talked about all the new ventures, briefly mentioning Governor Childress and his plan to widen the streets, refine a system of streetlights and improve the courts and prisons.

Amelia wondered if Virginia, the governor's daughter, and her daughter-in-law, had played a part in the governor's plans. She didn't bother asking since Wade was carrying on and on. There was hardly a chance to get a word in edgewise. As they reached Congress Avenue, he started in on the new capitol building which had been completed a few years before.

They stopped at the street corner to admire the capitol at the end of Congress Avenue.

"You might know that it took nine hundred men to build our lovely capitol," Wade said as he gazed down the busy road.

"I've heard that a time or two." Amelia smiled at the rapt expression on Wade's face. She turned back to study the grand structure, towering over the town of Austin. "I also heard it's taller than the capitol of Washington. We Texans can't resist showing off, can we?"

Amelia had grown up in Louisiana but considered herself Texan, or at least Texan enough to poke fun at the Lone Star

State. She spoke of showing off just to tease him, but he seemed not to notice.

He drew a deep sigh. The sight of the building pleased him deeply. "Of the nine hundred men, eighty-six came all the way from Scotland. Did you know?"

She shook her head but could guess where Wade was headed. She'd listened to both Wade and Robert McCord go on a time or two about their Scottish relatives. Robert loved to tell stories of his great-uncle stowing away on a sailing ship. Bartholomew McCord was just a boy of fourteen. He'd managed to hide himself on a ship bound for America, arriving with only a nickel in his pocket.

Amelia had heard the story so many times, she figured she knew it at least as well as Robert and Wade.

"The men came from Scotland?" she asked, suppressing a smile. "With just a few coins to their name?"

"No." Wade looked affronted. "They were hired as stonecutters. They were respected tradesmen. Not penniless immigrants."

Amelia patted his hand. "They did a fine job. With such a grand capitol, Texans can hold their head high."

"I'd like to think so," Wade murmured.

They crossed the busy road, Wade guiding her to the far side of the boulevard. When they reached the hotel, he kept a respectful distance as she spoke with the front desk. The young fellow manning the post eyed her dusty trousers and scuffed boots with thinly veiled disapproval as if doubting her right to stay in the McCord suite.

Amelia was about to give the young man a stern talking-to. She'd been on the road since sunrise and hadn't had a chance to wash away some of the dust and grit. Before she could give the young fellow a piece of her mind, Wade stepped in.

151

Wade gave the young fellow a dressing-down, insisting he mind his tongue. Apparently, Wade had more sway with the hotel staff than an unaccompanied scruffy female traveler. He blustered and threatened but managed to do both with a smile and cordial manner. That was Wade McCord. Still, Amelia had to admit she was impressed.

The young man relented. Before Wade was done, however, he demanded a supper reservation for two in the dining room that evening. *To make up for insulting the lady.*

It took Amelia a moment to realize Wade was referring to her. She was the insulted lady. Not only that, but she now had to get dolled up to eat in the Driskill's fussy, fancy dining room.

"Dang it," she muttered under her breath. "Probably going to have to wear a dress and act ladylike."

Chapter Twenty-Four
The Moment I First Saw You

Daisy

The morning storms abated around midday but returned a short time later. The sky darkened and the clouds opened up as the house shook with each roll of thunder. Poppy fretted about the violent weather. She followed Daisy around the house, yelping with each flash of lightning. At first, Daisy tried to comfort her youngest sister, but by midafternoon, her patience had worn thin.

"Give me a moment's peace, would you?" Daisy snapped as she ladled broth into a cup.

"I hate the storm," Poppy whined. "Usually, I make a pretend tea party for me and Mrs. Cavendish, but I left her with Mr. Honeycutt."

Daisy blew a strand of hair from her eyes. "What's Lilly doing?"

Poppy grimaced. "She's reading."

"Reading?" Daisy still wasn't used to her sister's newfound love of books. Perhaps it was better said that it was a love of one particular book, Uncle Horace's medical volume.

Poppy nodded. "She's reading about teeth."

"Teeth?"

Poppy hugged herself as she nodded.

"What do you mean?"

"Teeth!" Poppy looked resentful. "Problems with teeth! Things to do when someone has a toothache or a sore throat."

"Heaven help me," Daisy muttered as she set the bowl of broth on a plate.

"This morning she was reading about feet. What's a bunion?" Poppy asked. "Something people get from their shoes? That's what Lilly said. I wear shoes every day. Does that mean I'll get bunions?"

Daisy smiled at her sister's worried expression. She stroked her fingers along the girl's jaw and straightened the collar of her dress. "I don't think young girls need to worry about such things. It's more of an elderly person's concern."

She hoped to ease the girl's worry but instead her sister looked more fretful than before. "Poppy, don't worry. Even if you get a bunion one day, it won't be life-threatening."

Poppy's eyes clouded with worry. She clasped Daisy's hand in both of hers and gazed up with an earnest, longing expression. "Will Mr. Honeycutt be all right?"

Daisy's heart squeezed. Poppy was so young and yet had suffered a great deal. Their parents passed away. Uncle Horace passed away. Now Mr. Honeycutt lay in a bed down the hall fighting an infection.

Daisy could hardly bear to think of his wound, or how Poppy had found the gun. Or how she herself had accidentally fired it, injuring Mr. Honeycutt and then promptly neglecting his wound. A wave of nausea came over her. Thankfully, Poppy wandered out of the kitchen and saw none of her distress.

Leaning against the counter, Daisy did her best to collect her thoughts. All day, she'd prayed for Mr. Honeycutt's recovery and for forgiveness for her long list of mistakes.

She took the broth to his room, hoping he might be awake and well enough to take a little of the nourishing liquids. Several times that day, Lilly had read to her about the benefits of hearty broths. As expected, Lilly spent more time reading about hearty broths than actually preparing them, but that was nothing new.

Daisy knocked lightly on the door.

She waited. Even though she'd been in and out of Mr. Honeycutt's room many times over the course of the day, she didn't feel comfortable simply walking in. Usually, when she knocked, Mr. Honeycutt muttered some indistinct reply.

Not this time. This time his reply was a crisp, cheerful, startlingly lucid reply.

"Enter!"

Daisy blinked. She'd left him not more than two hours before, perspiring one minute, shivering the next, dozing fitfully, muttering about how to break wild mustangs, claiming that task was easier than running any logging outfit.

She spoke again. "Mr. Honeycutt?"

"C'mon in."

Cautiously, she pushed the door open and stepped inside. To her astonishment and great relief, Mr. Honeycutt sat up in bed looking neither chilled nor feverish. His eyes were bright. The blankets were piled around him in a twisted heap. Poppy's doll, Mrs. Cavendish, lay beside him, a sight that might have amused her if Mr. Honeycutt hadn't been so very ill just that morning.

She edged closer, setting the broth on a nearby table.

"I'm feeling much better," Mr. Honeycutt said. He smiled. "Mama always said a good hard sweat marked the end of an illness."

Daisy nodded. "Thank goodness."

Mr. Honeycutt folded his hands and eyed the tray. "I'm all better even though I've enjoyed you fussing over me, Daisy. What did you bring me?"

"Just a little..."

Her words drifted off as a mark on his face drew her attention. She bent down to study his unshaven jaw and try to figure out why he had such a curious mark on his cheek. Slowly, she lifted her hand and brushed her fingertips across the small, imprinted mark.

She lowered her gaze to the doll lying beside Mr. Honeycutt. Poor Mrs. Cavendish. She lay on her side, limbs askew, hair tousled, and bonnet slanted over one eye. Daisy let out a soft gasp of surprise as her attention drifted back to the peculiar mark on Mr. Honeycutt's grizzled cheek.

He frowned. "What's the matter?"

She straightened. What was the matter? How could she explain such a thing to a gruff, proud Texas cowboy? A man who ran not just the sawmill but the vast expanse of logging around Pineville. Biting her lip, she did her best to keep from smiling.

While Mr. Honeycutt wasn't bathed in sweat or suffering from a fever, he was showing evidence of sleeping with a child's doll. The imprint of Mrs. Cavendish's small, delicate hand was clear on the side of his unshaven jaw.

After everything that had happened over the last few days and all the worries and guilt and fear she'd endured, a wash of relief swept over her. Mr. Honeycutt, the man she'd accidentally shot and whose wound she'd forgotten to tend to, might just survive despite everything.

"What's wrong?" Mr. Honeycutt demanded.

"Nothing." Daisy held back a smile and handed him the cup of broth. "Nothing at all."

Mr. Honeycutt shook his head. "In the morning, first thing, I need to head to the mill."

Daisy felt her amusement fade. "Of course. You need to get back to work."

"I do. What's more, I feel mighty keen on making certain the Pineville townsfolk don't start talking about me staying in your home." He sobered.

The unrelenting rain drummed on the roof. Raindrops hit the window and rolled down the glass pane. Off in the distance, thunder rumbled. The storm had no end, or so it seemed to Daisy.

Her throat felt tight as she considered Mr. Honeycutt's words. He worried about the townsfolk talking. His concerns were well founded. Folk liked to talk, especially in Pineville. Just the same, she couldn't imagine they'd find out about him staying with her.

"That's the main thing." Mr. Honeycutt said in a resolute tone. "I don't care for folks talking about the Muldoon girls, especially *my* Muldoon girl."

Her heart shook. His girl? His girl...

"I'm not your girl, Mr. Honeycutt." She retreated a step. "Please don't say such things. I'm no one's girl. Not while I have younger sisters who need my attention."

"All right," he replied quietly.

Warmth rose to her cheeks. She cupped her hands to her face as if that might chase away the color. It didn't help that Mr. Honeycutt watched her with a tender and caring look. If only he'd stop. And yet, she had to admit she liked the way he gazed at her. It was the first time in her life a man had regarded her with such warmth in his eyes.

"I'm very sorry, Daisy," he said. "Forgive me."

"I confess that I enjoy the attention. I'm not proud of that. Especially when you've promised your heart to another."

"Daisy..." his words trailed off. "The situation is not what it seems."

She stopped him with an upturned hand. "Please."

He shook his head, tossed aside the blankets, and rose from the bed. Alarmed, Daisy backed away, stopping when her back hit the door. He turned away and moved to the window where he stood in the dull gray light, staring through the rain-streaked windows.

"I always figured I'd marry one day." He frowned as he studied the gloomy day. "I figured I'd meet a girl, court her and ask for her when I knew she was the one."

"Please, stop."

He sighed. "I was sort of surprised when it happened in reverse."

"What do you mean?"

He turned. A smile tugged at his lips. "I mean, that I knew you were the one before anything else. I knew the moment I first saw you."

The moment I first saw you...

Her heart thudded a hard, steady drum against her ribs. Turmoil churned inside her heart. Frustration too. He was engaged to be married. How could he say such mocking words to her? He was a kind, decent man, or so she thought, and yet, he toyed with her heart.

As her distress grew with each passing second, her mouth went dry, making it near impossible to summon a response. Worse, her eyes stung with tears. Oh, how she hated to cry in front of others. Silently, she prayed that she might hold back her foolish tears.

After a long moment, she managed to subdue her anguish. Her heartbeat slowed. Her turmoil ebbed. The threat of tears passed. She lifted her chin and spoke, her voice hardly trembling. "I'm greatly relieved that you're feeling better, Mr. Honeycutt."

Mr. Honeycutt seemed lost in thought as he directed his attention on some point off toward the misty horizon. She'd expected him to say something taunting or roguish. Before he could torment her further, she turned on her heel and hurried out of the room.

Chapter Twenty-Five
Dinner at the Driskill

Amelia

Amelia was shown to Robert and Sophie's rooms. Servants milled around, settling her belongings, ordering a tray of refreshments, and drawing a hot bath. They fussed endlessly until Amelia lost her patience and sent them from her room to leave her in peace and quiet.

Once they were gone, she stripped off her clothes. The simple act of taking off her shirt and trousers made her feel a sight cleaner. She tossed them aside, fully intending to put them back on in the morning even if they were caked in grit and dust.

She sank into the warm, comforting bathwater. As much as she wanted to get to East Texas, she had to admit how much she relished the fine accommodations right there in Austin. She'd intended to make the trip as quickly as possible but hadn't had any more nightmares. Surely, she decided, her bad dream meant nothing more than just that – a bad dream.

The dreams were likely due to Zach being away from home. Even though he was a grown man, she still saw him as the baby. Zach was her youngest. He'd always be her baby. She loved Daniel and Simon, of course, but Zach held a special spot in her heart. When she gave birth to Zach, she'd been newly widowed. She felt a bond with Zach that she didn't share with the other two.

As she soaked in the hot bath, she decided her bad dreams were nothing more than maternal fretfulness. Like all three boys, Zach was smart, strong, and capable. He was fine. Just fine. That's what she told herself.

After she bathed, she got out and dried off with a large, soft, lavender-scented towel. Next, she wrapped herself in one of Sophie's silken bathrobes and searched the gowns hanging in the wardrobe. Amelia knew Sophie would encourage her to take what she wanted. If anything, Sophie would be offended if she didn't avail herself of the various gowns.

The empty apartment seemed quiet and lonesome. Amelia had never stayed at the Driskill without Sophie and Robert and had to admit it wasn't nearly as much fun without friends. Robert was always quiet, but always near, ready to tend to anything either of "his girls" needed.

And Sophie always chattered endlessly about this or that, mostly in English but occasionally in French. At times, her chatter wore on Amelia. Now, though, in the quiet of the late afternoon, as the shadows lengthened across the empty rooms, Amelia dearly missed her friends.

"It can't be helped," she said aloud as if trying to console herself. "Next time I come to Austin, I'll come with the rest of the pesky McCords."

With that in mind, Amelia searched Sophie's walnut armoire. She eyed the various gowns and finally chose a dress of pale blue silk with an embroidered bodice, leg-o-mutton sleeves, and full, gored skirt. If Sophie were there, she'd probably declare the gown all wrong, but Amelia wasn't going to worry about Sophie's disapproval.

Amelia might have made a poor choice, but she was in Austin. Far from home. She wasn't likely to run into anyone she knew.

Pinned to the gown was a matching hat, adorned with aigrettes. It was pretty. Amelia could picture the hat perched on Sophie's head, beneath her carefully coifed locks. Amelia suspected that the delicate hat could be entirely too much trouble. She was used to her trusty Stetson.

After a full quarter-hour struggling with the hat, Amelia tossed it aside with disgust. Instead, she resolved to attend dinner with her hair done in a simple arrangement, coiled neatly at the base of her neck.

"It's just Wade McCord," she muttered to her reflection. "He's a nice enough fellow, but I'm not trying to impress anyone."

She winced at her plain appearance and picked through Sophie's jewelry box. A necklace might help matters. Maybe some earbobs. Amelia owned a few pairs, old pieces from when she was a girl. She hadn't worn them in years and didn't even know where they were anymore. It seemed awkward to even consider the matter. What sort of color gem should she choose? Should it match the dress, or should it contrast?

The entire ordeal of getting ready for supper, especially without the help of Sophie, seemed like entirely too much trouble. She wished she could simply avoid the matter. If only she could order a tray and eat alone.

Before she could decide, Wade knocked at the door. She flung the door open, as if it was the door's fault for confusing her about matters about dresses, hairstyles and jewelry.

Wade stood on the other side of the door, looking calm, cool and composed. His relaxed, bemused expression only served to irritate her further.

"What?" she demanded. Remembering her manners, she toned down her harsh response. "Pardon me," she said from between gritted teeth. "I meant to say hello." She ran her palms down the front of the dress.

He chuckled.

She made another attempt to greet him with a civil tone as she stepped across the threshold. "Good evening, Wade."

Wade eyed her fancy attire with a look of astonishment and clear admiration. Amelia noted a glimmer of satisfaction. She had no interest in Wade McCord. None. Still, she had to admit it felt nice to have a handsome man regard her with appreciation.

Wade, ever the jokester, recovered from his surprise. He clapped his hand over his heart and staggered back. "Amelia?" He frowned and looked bewildered. "Amelia *Honeycutt?*"

"Oh, Wade, hush already."

He smiled and laughed softly but held his tongue.

Amelia noted, with some resentment, his flawless attire, his freshly pressed suit, and white, crisply ironed shirt. Even his tie looked perfect. He'd taken the time to shave. He'd carefully combed his hair. He looked fresh as a daisy. She wondered if he might have had time to nap. Maybe. Probably while she agonized over the dresses stuffed in Sophie's armoire.

Had this man spent the day riding a dusty road? The same trail she'd ridden?

"Shall we?" he asked gallantly.

"I suppose," she grumbled.

He took her arm in his and escorted her downstairs. She spoke of his being a bit of a dandy. He spoke of how she was always lovely no matter what she wore. If she wore trousers and a Stetson or if she dressed in fine silk, she always stole his breath. Amelia resisted the urge to tell him he was an idiot. His pretty words meant nothing to her.

Despite her irritation, Amelia had to admit she enjoyed not only his flattery but also the fine meal they shared. Wade proved every bit the gentleman, ordering dinner for her even though she was perfectly capable of picking out her own meal. To start, he requested consommé, followed by a small filet with cauliflower au gratin and salad with herbs. For dessert, he ordered a slice of lemon pie.

"We can share," he told the attendant.

Amelia laughed and shook her head. "I don't know, Wade. Sharing dessert? That could try the bonds of our friendship."

Wade recoiled with exaggerated concern, smiled, and told the waiter to bring two slices.

Amelia was about to confess just how much she was enjoying the brief stay in Austin when she heard a familiar voice.

"Why, is that Amelia Honeycutt?"

A jolt of surprise stole her breath as she scanned the dining room. To her dismay, Orville Childress threaded his way through the crowd, a smug smile on his lips.

"Hello, Orville," she managed.

He smirked. "So nice to run into my favorite in-law here at the Driskill Hotel. And look at this, Amelia Honeycutt dining with Wade McCord. I recall seeing the two of you at the governor's mansion before I won my re-election."

"That's right," Wade said. "I escorted Mrs. Honeycutt that evening, the night Simon proposed to Virginia."

Orville waved off his words. "As I recall, you both swore the evening was an isolated event. Just a one-time outing. Is that right?"

He chuckled as if answering his own question.

Amelia felt warmth rush to her face. Rarely did she feel any sense of embarrassment, but Orville's voice traveled, and she could tell he'd caught the attention of a fair number of guests there in the Driskill dining room. While she didn't know any of the guests, she didn't especially care to be the subject of their interest.

Wade nodded with a good-natured smile. "How are things at the governor's mansion? I've heard you're quite fond of the lady running your kitchen. Edith, is it?"

Orville paled.

Amelia leaned in, wondering where the discussion might lead. "Who's Edith?"

"I'd like to know as well," Wade said cheerfully. "Who exactly is Edith?"

Orville tugged his jacket over his expansive midsection. He lifted his chin to give them a haughty glare. "I hope you enjoy your evening."

"Thank you," Wade replied.

"Amelia," Orville said stiffly. "I believe I'm joining you for lunch in a few weeks' time."

Orville looked so uncomfortable that Amelia was suddenly pleased they'd ended up staying the night at the Driskill. She didn't dislike her son's father-in-law. Not exactly. Orville was trying his best. Still, the man aggravated her at times. And she didn't appreciate his attempt to embarrass her in the middle of the Driskill dining room.

"A few weeks' time," she mused. "That's right. How could I forget?"

Orville looked slighted.

"I can't wait to see you again," Amelia said airily. "Feel free to bring Edith."

Orville curled his lip, tugged his sleeves down and turned on his heel to stalk off. He crossed the dining room, pausing here and there to chat with various patrons. He'd quickly reverted to the charming, small-town, Bethany Springs native son, twice-elected governor.

Amelia couldn't hold back a soft round of laughter. Orville Childress. He was still a rascal, still full of himself and he still inspired the worst in her. As he shuffled across the dining room, she wondered how Orville Childress managed to father a daughter as sweet, kind, and noble as Virginia.

Still, despite her irritation with her old nemesis, she felt some small glimmer of happiness on his behalf. He was impossible. Annoying and entirely too full of himself, and yet, it was a fine thing if a man of his age and standing could find a nice lady friend. Men did better with a feminine influence. They were a tad vulnerable in that regard. Men needed a wife to tend to them probably because they weren't as sturdy and strong-willed as women.

Of that, Amelia Honeycutt was quite sure.

Chapter Twenty-Six
Lilly and Poppy Deliver Lunch

Zach

By the following morning, Zach felt as hale and hearty as ever and left the cottage early. With a twinge of guilt, he slipped away, like a thief in the night as the Muldoon girls slept. He arrived at the mill just after dawn. The rain had slowed enough that there existed a chance the loggers would return to work. Much depended on the roads and if the oxen could pull their immense loads.

Sitting in his office, he worked by lamplight, making plans for improving the roads. The matter of good roads wasn't anything he'd had to contend with on the ranch. The longhorns weren't troubled by mud. Then again, they weren't pulling tons of raw lumber.

If he could work out some plans, he'd write his mother a letter explaining his idea. He was woefully behind in his correspondence with Mama. She'd written several times and he could bet her next letter would have a few lines chiding him. A pang of homesickness struck his heart. He wasn't too proud to admit that he missed his home and family.

After the men arrived, the mill sprang to life. They fired up the various saws and began work even though the lumber deliveries had been slowed by the rain. The scent of pine resin filled the air.

He made the rounds, checking on the men's work, keeping a wary eye on the big saw, grateful that it ran without any trouble. Late morning, Lilly and Poppy arrived with a basket. He ushered the girls up the stairs to his office, away from the noise and dust.

"Daisy sent lunch," Lilly said, as she set food and a jar of lemonade on his desk. "She said she was too busy to come and asked me."

"Is it always so noisy?" Poppy asked.

"All day," Zach said. "Sometimes when I leave, my ears are ringing." He shoved his hands into his pockets. "I didn't expect either of you to make the trip down to the mill."

"We worried you might be hungry," Poppy explained.

"I wanted to check your shoulder." Lilly eyed him matter-of-factly. "And to tell you that whatever you told my sister has her out of sorts."

He lifted a brow.

Lilly narrowed her eyes. "Daisy doesn't anger easily. What did you say?"

Poppy sat quietly, listening intently.

Zach smiled sheepishly as he unwrapped one of the sandwiches. "I care for Daisy."

Lilly waved her hand impatiently. "What did you *tell* her?"

An unwelcome wave of warmth burned his chest and rose along the length of his neck. He coughed. Set the sandwich aside and coughed a little more. When his coughing subsided, he tried to clear his throat with a swallow of lemonade, but the tart drink set off another round of sputtering.

Lilly rolled her eyes as she tugged the ribbons of her bonnet. With a brisk gesture, she directed him to the nearby chair and muttered a few words about his wound and rummaged through the basket. She allowed him some measure of peace to recover from his coughing spell. With a look of clear disapproval, she glanced around the office. "I'm not sure I want to tend to your injury in such unsanitary conditions."

"What's unsanitary?" Poppy asked.

"Filthy," Lilly answered.

The small girl wrinkled her nose and nodded.

He chuckled as he sat back in the chair.

"What's so funny?" Lilly demanded.

"You even sound like a nurse. A bossy nurse, one that will likely scare patients."

Poppy laughed. Seeing her sister's irritation, she tried to cover her smile with her hand.

"What I am is a concerned sister," Lilly snapped. "Does your shoulder hurt?"

Frowning, Zach rolled his shoulders. "No, come to think of it."

Lilly regarded him thoughtfully and very gently, she set her hand over the bandage. "I don't detect any heat or inflammation."

Poppy sat up straight. "What's-"

"Swelling," Lilly replied. "Inflammation means swelling and it's not a good sign. Heat indicates an infection."

Poppy nodded but remained silent.

Zach sighed. "I'm sure it's fine, Lilly."

"I'll change the dressing this evening. It would be best to leave the bandage undisturbed here in the mill." She sniffed as she returned her supplies to the basket.

Zach straightened his shirt. "Lilly, what if my family could help you with nursing school? Would you like to attend?"

Her prim expression fell away as she lifted her gaze. He glimpsed a flicker of uncertainty behind her eyes. She shrugged a shoulder and looked dismayed.

"You might like it," he offered. "In fact, I'm sure you already like it."

Lilly shook her head. "I don't know if I could manage. I'm not the smart one in the family."

Her words left him too surprised to reply.

She went on. "My sister, Daisy, has always been the smart one. Before our parents passed away, they intended to send her off to become a teacher. She always did so well in school. Not me. Or at least not as well as Daisy."

He smiled and leaned back in his chair. Crossing his arms, he shook his head with a mix of amusement and sympathy. Somewhere along the line, this young lady had begun to think poorly of herself. It came as a surprise, especially since she seemed to carry herself with confidence.

"You and your sisters are named after flowers." He smiled gently. "Maybe you, Lilly, are the late bloomer."

A smile tugged at her lips. "Maybe. You're very kind. But I can't imagine passing the entrance exam. I left school two years ago."

"You might just surprise yourself."

She waved off his words. Still, he could tell she held back a smile. Packing up her belongings, she got ready to leave. Poppy followed them out of the office.

Zach went with them. He didn't want the girls to leave unaccompanied, traipse past all the workers or overhear their rough language. They descended the steps and turned to the large front door.

When they reached the door, he thanked the girls for the sandwich. Before saying goodbye, he offered a few gentle words to Lilly. "Don't deny your gifts, Lilly-the-late-bloomer."

Poppy snickered.

Lilly tied her bonnet and tried mightily to frown at him. Despite her best efforts, a smile curved her lips. "Fine. I won't. And in return I ask that you keep from upsetting my sister."

He lifted his hand in mock salute. "Yes, ma'am."

"She's never been sweet on a fellow before." Lilly's eyes clouded with worry. "Daisy acts like she can take on the world but deep down she's the most tenderhearted person I know. I won't stand by and watch her get hurt."

"I understand." Zach set his hand over his heart. "The last thing I want is to hurt anyone, especially Daisy. She's all I think about. I just want to care for her. Protect her."

Lilly drew a sharp breath of surprise. Poppy eyed him with surprise as well. He couldn't help feeling a little shocked himself. He waited for some sign of approval, as if he were asking for permission to court Lilly's sister. After a moment or two of consideration, Lilly's eyes lit with a happy, albeit mischievous glint. She laughed softly and bid him good-bye.

Poppy followed suit and skipped after her sister.

After the girls left, he wandered back into the mill, his mind preoccupied with Daisy. He'd upset her. He suspected as much yesterday. Somehow, hearing the words said aloud from Lilly troubled him twice as much.

Guilt squeezed his heart.

How could he make amends? Without breaking things off with Marie, he had no chance with Daisy. Marie was likely halfway across the ocean. Even if he sent Marie a letter, it would be months before he received a reply.

Time was of the essence. He noted a sense of urgency. He wanted to court Daisy, to show her he was sincere, but understood the importance of moving quickly. She and her sisters were vulnerable, especially here in Pineville.

He and his brothers shared that same sentiment, that of protecting others. How Daniel and Simon came to value that outlook, he couldn't say. For him, it came about when he was just a boy of ten when he'd gotten kicked in the ribs by some rank mule. He'd lain in bed for days, his ribs cracked or broken, every breath painful.

One night, he stirred from his sleep. To his surprise, his mother sat in a chair by his bed. She wept. Her shoulders shook as she sobbed. It was the first time he'd seen his mother cry. He'd never imagined that his injury might cause his mother or anyone else to suffer. Her suffering affected him deeply.

From that moment on, he began to think of matters differently. He grew fond of finding small ways of caring for certain folks, especially his family, his mother and older brothers. As he grew older, he saw other ways he might lend a hand to those in need. When he joined the Bethany Brotherhood, that notion of protecting others grew even stronger.

He wanted to care for Daisy, to be sure. He wanted to shield her from trouble, but he wanted more. He wanted to sit down each evening at the end of the long day, hold her hand to say grace over a good meal. He wanted to brush stray locks from her eyes or make her laugh and so much more. It came as no surprise that what he really wanted was to have and to hold Daisy Muldoon.

Forever.

He winced. The idea wasn't going to go over well with the eldest Muldoon girl. Not at all. He pondered his dilemma as a heavily loaded oxcart rolled up to the back door.

Jonas came to his side as Zach watched workers unload the cart. "The men were talking about that Lilly Muldoon coming to the mill."

Zach narrowed his eyes. "Watch your step, Jonas. I care about the Muldoon girls."

Jonas held up his hands. "I'm not trying to cause trouble. I just thought you should know some of the men get to bragging. They talk about how one day they'll catch Lilly or Daisy and steal a kiss. Some say more but I'd rather not repeat that sort of thing."

Zach bristled.

Jonas looked apologetic. "I meant no disrespect, sir. Just thought you'd like to know. Truly."

"Much obliged," Zach replied gruffly.

Matt Jonas's words shouldn't have surprised him. Zach had already dealt with this very matter of untoward attention. Just the same, it troubled him. He felt more determined than ever to help the three Muldoon girls. Lilly ought to have the chance to become a nurse if that's what called to her. Little Poppy ought to be in school too. The problem was there weren't any in Pineville. Daisy should... well, he liked to think Daisy belonged by his side.

Despite the trouble facing him in the form of a stubborn, fair-haired girl, and regardless how much she might argue and complain every step of the way, he vowed to care for Daisy. Not just Daisy, but all the pesky, troublesome, utterly charming, impossible Muldoon girls.

Soon.

Chapter Twenty-Seven
That Mr. Honeycutt

Daisy

Daisy spent the morning cleaning the back room where Mr. Honeycutt had stayed. She wanted to rid the room of any sign of his fever or recovery. She felt it was the least she could do. She swept the floor and mopped. Next, she would scrub the bedsheets.

He was back at work, spending long hours at the mill and would likely return to the cottage hungry and tired. He'd appreciate freshly laundered bed linens when he turned in this evening. It gave her something to do with her nervous energy, something that would count in some small way in making amends for the trouble she'd caused him.

Poppy appeared from the side door, her small face flushed. The trip to the mercantile was more difficult than usual. The afternoon sun had warmed up considerably, and the air was heavy with the prior days' rains. That and the inch of mud caked on her shoes had surely made the trip taxing.

Poppy had gone to the mercantile alone.

Earlier, while Lilly and Poppy had been checking on Mr. Honeycutt, Daisy realized there were some things she needed for the evening meal. She'd asked Lilly to go to the mercantile, but Lilly claimed she was far too busy. Doing what, she didn't say, but Daisy suspected her sister just wanted to read about various medical complaints. So, Poppy went alone.

Daisy fed the sheets through the wringer. "Did you manage to buy all the items on my list?"

"Everything but the cardamom," Poppy said. "Mr. Cook said he won't have any till Christmas. Can I help wring the sheet?"

Daisy nodded and together the two girls turned the crank. Uncle Horace had been one of the first in all of Pineville to get a wringer. As a bachelor, he'd found washing his laundry tiresome and relished any time-saving tool. Daisy well-remembered the task of twisting laundry by hand when she was a young girl and was grateful that she didn't have that chore to contend with anymore.

Even better, laundry dried in half the time, although with the day's wet air, it would be hours before she'd clear the line. Poppy loved turning the wringer's crank, and she smiled as the rollers squeezed the excess water from the fabric.

Daisy unraveled the bedsheet and shook it out before hanging it on the line. "I can do without cardamom, I suppose. Did Mr. Cook bring you home?"

"He did."

Daisy smiled as she pinned the sheet on the line. A breeze stirred across the linen, rippling the snowy white expanse in the bright sunshine. "That's so kind. Mr. Cook is very sweet, looking out for us whenever he can. I felt badly sending you on your own. You've never shopped for the family until today. You're such a grown-up girl."

Poppy wandered to the laundry line and traced a fingertip along the edge of a kitchen towel as it fluttered gently. "Mr. Cook didn't seem so sweet when we chatted on the way home. He seemed perturbed."

"What do you mean?"

"He seemed very stern. His face was dark and angry-looking."

Daisy hung another kitchen towel. "Perhaps he and Mrs. Cook had quarreled."

"I don't think so."

"Maybe he didn't receive an order of turnips."

Daisy bit back a smile. Poppy disliked turnips and would likely find the comment amusing. But no. Poppy didn't smile. The girl seemed lost in thought as she wandered the length of the laundry line.

"Or apples," Daisy offered.

"He seemed mad, but not about turnips. And not about apples."

Daisy let out a huff. "Why not simply tell me instead of keeping me guessing? I have other chores I need to attend to and don't believe Lilly plans on helping. So, spill the beans."

Poppy whirled around, her face reddening. "He's mad about Mr. Honeycutt staying in our home. There. Now you know. I'm not certain what I said wrong, because he was so very angry!"

Daisy held a towel up ready to pin it to the line. Poppy's words sent a jolt down her spine.

"You told him about Mr. Honeycutt?"

Poppy nodded, trying to look defiant as her eyes filled with tears.

Daisy felt her blood drain to her feet. Poppy had told Pineville's grocer about Mr. Honeycutt staying in their home. She'd talked about the one thing Daisy hoped to keep a secret. Of course, she had. After all, Daisy hadn't told her sister to keep it to herself. She could hardly blame the girl.

Daisy slowly lowered the towel and turned to face her sister. For a long moment, she stared, unable to speak, her mind working through all the bad things she'd tried to avoid since Uncle Horace had died. Everything that could ruin her or her sisters.

Shame. Disgrace. Dishonor.

Finally, she managed to ask, "Mr. Honeycutt? He's mad about Mr. Honeycutt?"

Poppy nodded. "He didn't know. He seemed very surprised and very mad."

"Oh. Heavens."

"I don't know why he got so... so furious. What's wrong with Mr. Honeycutt staying here, especially after you shot him in the shoulder? I asked Mr. Cook that question, but he didn't understand. He got even more upset and mixed up."

Daisy's legs shook beneath her. She sank to her knees. This was the very thing she'd feared ever since her uncle had passed. If the loggers of Pineville suspected she allowed men to stay in her home, her family's honor would be lost. Some would start thinking about how they might charm Lilly into sharing her favors. How on earth could she protect her sister from the wildfire that Poppy had accidentally sparked?

Poppy crouched beside her, sniffling and trying to sound cheerful as she stroked Daisy's hair. "He had other deliveries to make but said he's plans to pay a visit to settle things with Mr. Honeycutt. To make things right."

"Settle things with Mr. Honeycutt?"

Poppy nodded. "Actually, he said he'd settle things with *that* Mr. Honeycutt."

"Oh," Daisy murmured. "Oh, dear."

"He said something else." Poppy hiccupped. "Something I didn't understand because it didn't make sense."

"Yes?"

"He said that when he comes to settle things with that Mr. Honeycutt, he's bringing a preacher."

Chapter Twenty-Eight
The Agreeable Groom

Zach

As the day wore on, the mill grew busier. The sun had been shining since dawn, which had dried the roadways considerably, allowing the oxen to draw their heavy loads to the sawmill. The men unloaded the logs and kept the saws humming. Zach circled the mill, checking the growing stacks of finished lumber and counting the wagonloads of raw timber.

Work progressed well. As the sun sank past the horizon, Zach ordered the men to shut down operations. One by one, the saws slowed to a standstill. The workers set off for home. Zach shut his office door and locked up the mill. He rode to the cottage as the moon rose in the east, casting a lovely, silvery light through the thick growth of trees.

A soft breeze stirred the piney woods. As he took in the peaceful evening, he considered the notion that Pineville was pretty. He'd admit as much, but Pineville was nowhere as pretty as Bethany Springs. Nothing compared to home. Not as far as he was concerned.

He passed a pair of riders heading to town. They acknowledged him with a curt nod. In the next instant, they resumed a conversation about various unsavory topics. It seemed that the men who lived in logging towns gravitated to that sort of talk. Just one more reason to stay on with the

Muldoon girls for as long as possible. If he stayed the nights in the back room, he'd be able to protect the girls from unwanted attention.

He rode the last stretch before the cottage, noting the sound of people gathered ahead. Frowning, he urged his horse into a lope. A strong need to reach the cottage came over him, an urge to make certain Daisy and her sisters were well.

Drawing near to the cottage, he noted various townsfolk, their forms illuminated by lamplight. They gathered in front of the cottage. In the shadowed light, he could make out close to a dozen. His chest tightened. He prayed the girls were safe. In the same breath he chided himself for lingering at the mill. He ought to have returned to the cottage earlier instead of working late.

He drew up his horse, tied the gelding to the hitching post and hurried to the cottage. "Something wrong?" he demanded of the one of the observers.

"Darned right something's wrong." In the flickering lamplight, Zach noted the man's deeply etched scowl. "Some fellow has been troubling the Muldoon girls."

Zach's heart plummeted. He crossed the porch, pushing through the throng. Daisy met him at the door, pale and stricken.

"Zach," she whispered. "You're here."

She glanced past him and grimaced before turning her attention back to him.

He clasped her shoulders. "What's happened? Is everyone all right?"

"What happened?" Daisy squeezed her eyes shut for a long moment before continuing. "What happened is I sent Poppy to the store."

"Poppy?" he asked, his voice choking.

"She's fine. She's completely fine."

He said nothing. Instead, he waited for her to go on. His heart hammered steadily against his ribs. Distantly, he noted the angry murmurings of the crowd. They seemed agitated. He tried as best he could to ignore their fervor.

"You see, Poppy went to the store."

"You said that already." He shook her shoulders, a gentle movement but one that earned him a cry of indignation from the crowd.

Daisy went on. "She talked to Mr. Cook."

"Right. Of course. And then what happened? Is she sick?"

Daisy shook her head. "No. She told him that you're staying here, in the spare room at the back of the cottage. She explained that you were hurt. I don't think Mr. Cook believed that. He talked to others who doubted the notion as well. And now they probably doubt the entire story even more. Especially since you just rode up to the house, you see."

Zach dropped his hands from her shoulders and stepped back, suddenly aware of how his actions might appear to the crowd. The small town of Pineville would not take kindly to him being so forward with Daisy Muldoon.

The townsfolk wouldn't care that his family owned the mill. In fact, that might put him in a less favorable light. The citizens of Pineville would be most concerned with how he'd taken liberties, for that's how they would see things. The folks who lived in Pineville might not abide by rules of polite company, but they'd make sure strangers did. Especially around the town's young ladies.

The town's grocer strode from the crowd, his eyes full of judgment and menace. "You're going to do the right thing, mister."

The crowd gave a collective outcry. Some raised their fists. Others shook their heads and muttered vague threats.

Zach nodded. They wanted him to do the right thing? Well, that was just fine by him. He nodded in agreement. "All right."

Another man followed behind. "We're not going to abide by any sort of shenanigans."

Shenanigans...

"I don't approve of shenanigans," Zach said calmly.

Next came a gray-haired lady, a widow who worked at the post office. She shook her fist and let loose with a volley of language Zach had never heard from a woman's lips. Not even his mother on her worst day said such things.

Daisy let out a soft huff of surprise.

"You're going to marry her," Mr. Cook proclaimed.

The crowd shouted in unison.

Zach smiled. The entire evening had suddenly taken a very different, very unlikely turn. He liked it. He liked it a great deal. "If you insist."

And now it was Daisy who gripped his shoulders. "Mr. Honeycutt. Please. This is just a misunderstanding. I'm sure we can explain matters. Perhaps if we tell them how I shot you."

A gasp came from the crowd.

Zach waved a dismissive hand. "It was an accident."

Daisy nodded. "It could have been worse."

The crowd spoke amongst themselves and amid the confusion, a young man was pushed to the fore. He looked bewildered. A strand of hair fell over his eyes, and he hastily swiped it aside. He held a Bible in one hand and with a pained expression opened it to a clutch of handwritten pages.

He cleared his throat. "Dearly beloved..."

Zach's breath caught in his throat. He could tell there was no going back, not without inciting a small uproar. As his surprise gave way and he managed to draw a breath, he felt a smile begin to tug at the corners of his lips. It looked like he was getting married, by golly.

Zach clasped Daisy's hand in his and drew her close. She looked terrified.

The preacher was all wrong about things. He clearly assumed Zach would not want to marry. The rest of the crowd would think that too. Of course, they would. Zach didn't care. Not one bit. If this preacher had come to the cottage, intent on marrying him and Daisy, Zach wasn't going to object. Marriage was the perfect solution. He'd say his vows and from that moment forward, he'd take care of his sweet Daisy and her two sisters.

Chapter Twenty-Nine
Lilly Consoles (and teases) Daisy

Daisy

The day which had started out perfectly fine had ended on an unexpected note that resulted in her sharing vows with Zach Honeycutt.

Marriage vows...

After the minister pronounced them man and wife, Zach lowered to brush a kiss across her lips. Daisy had been too astonished to respond.

Zach smiled at her before turning to speak to the crowd. He assured Mr. Cook that nothing untoward had occurred, but he appreciated the man's concern. Next, Zach calmed the widow from the post office with a promise to take good care of the Muldoon girls, not just Daisy.

Lilly and Poppy came to her side to murmur soft words of support. They helped her inside so she might recover her wits away from the curious stares of the Pineville citizens. Daisy spent the next part of the evening tending to her chores in a sort of stupor. Mr. Honeycutt remained outside, thankfully.

For weeks, Daisy had spent her days and nights fretting about Lilly ending up in this sort of predicament. She'd envisioned all manner of disasters, all of which ended up with her younger sister marrying a man from Pineville.

Lilly prepared a quick meal of eggs and toast.

The four of them ate mostly in silence. Not even Poppy said much. Lilly simply asked people if they cared for more food. Daisy hardly tasted hers.

Mr. Honeycutt excused himself from the table when he was finished. "Dinner was very good. Thank you. I need to check on my horse. I'll bed down in the back bedroom. As usual."

Daisy knew the words were directed at her and nodded, glancing up to meet his gaze. "That'd be fine, Mr. Honeycutt."

His lips quirked. His eyes held a gentle warmth. Was it sympathy? She cringed inwardly.

He took his hat from the hook by the door and went outside to tend to his chores. Daisy could hardly eat. When dinner was done, Lilly and Poppy shoed her from the table, telling her they'd tidy the kitchen and wash the dishes.

Alone, in her room later that night, she undressed and donned one of her flannel gowns. The cottage was silent, her senses were heightened. Usually, she paid attention to her sisters' movements in the cottage. But tonight, her attention fixed on those of Mr. Honeycutt. She heard nothing.

The only sound came later when her sister knocked softly at the door. Lilly let herself into the room and shut the door quietly behind her.

"Poppy chatted with Mr. Honeycutt about puppies. She thinks she'll get one now that you and he are married. I checked his shoulder, changed the dressing and applied a fresh bandage." Lilly's tone was solemn just as it had been the past few days. Daisy had to admire how seriously Lilly regarded her duties.

Before Daisy could reply, Lilly went on, this time with a tone of amusement.

"His wound is improving." She smiled gently. "Marriage seems to agree with your husband."

Daisy squeezed her eyes shut and shuddered. "I'm sure he went through with things for the sake of appearances."

Lilly crossed the room and sat beside her. The two girls sat quietly. Daisy appreciated her sister's restraint. When Lilly took her hand and clasped it in hers, she leaned close and rested her head on Lilly's shoulder.

Usually, it was Daisy who consoled Lilly, unless she was consoling Poppy, of course. Daisy didn't care to be on the receiving end of sisterly comfort, but allowed herself a small, fleeting moment of vulnerability. The day's events warranted that.

"You care for him," Lilly whispered.

Daisy winced. She squeezed Lilly's hand. She did care for him. Her feelings went far more than simply caring but she could hardly bring herself to say the words aloud.

"It's all right." Lilly leaned closer. "Zach Honeycutt is a good man. In fact, he might even be good enough to deserve my sweet sister."

"Mr. Honeycutt is a fine man, but he's engaged."

Lilly didn't reply. She didn't even flinch. Instead, she wrapped her arm around Daisy's shoulders and held her in a gentle, comforting embrace.

Daisy lifted her head, knit her brow, and directed a pointed look at her sister. "Engaged. Engaged to be married."

Lilly snorted inelegantly. "Not anymore."

"What?"

"I'm no legal scholar but I don't believe a man can be both married *and* engaged."

"The Honeycutt family lives in a different world than the Muldoons. Just as soon as Mr. Honeycutt can discreetly put an end to this marriage, I'm certain he'll do just that. He's known his fiancée since they were both children. He's not going to discard her just because Mr. Cook stormed down here to demand Mr. Honeycutt do the right thing."

Lilly's smile widened. "Often when I tend to his wound, he's quiet, lost in thought. Other times he visits and ask all sorts of things. Goodness, it's like twenty questions."

Daisy tried not to look resentful. Every male in the county wanted to visit with Lilly. Daisy hardly needed reminding.

"The questions are always about you. What were you like as a child? Were you cheerful? Were you pensive? I tell him you were both cheerful and pensive. What sorts of things do you especially like? Yesterday, he seemed to want to buy you a gift."

Daisy listened, hardly daring to believe her sister's words. "A gift?"

Lilly nodded. She drew her features taut and did her best to look fierce. She lowered her voice an octave, to produce her best impression of Mr. Honeycutt's voice. "Tell me a little about your sister, Daisy, and what she enjoys. What sorts of things does she especially like? Pretty dresses? Jewelry?"

Lilly snorted again, only this time a little louder. "I keep telling him that most girls enjoy both dresses and jewels, but my sister Daisy prefers books. Then he grumbled because there's no bookstore in Pineville. How can he buy you a gift if there aren't any proper shops in this tiny logging town? I pointed out all three of us, you, me and Poppy, enjoy candy and there's a candy counter at the mercantile, but I don't think he was listening. Next, he asked about jewels. Were you fond of anything in particular?"

"Jewels." Daisy spoke quietly. "I've never owned jewelry."

Lilly sighed. "Things can change."

"Don't you see? Muldoons don't marry Honeycutts." Daisy sprang to her feet and paced the room. "I've got to find the money Uncle Horace hid. It's more urgent than ever. Getting my hands on the money is the only way I can get the three of us out of Pineville, and the only way I can release Mr. Honeycutt from this terrible predicament."

Lilly shrugged a slim shoulder. She rose from the bed and casually strolled to the door, a smile playing on her lips. Stopping in the doorway, she bid Daisy a cheerful good night. "I suppose you'll spend your wedding night right here in the very room you always sleep in."

Daisy's face burned with mortification. She opened her mouth to reply. Finding no response, she closed her mouth. It shocked and pained Daisy that her younger sister spoke so lightly of a wedding night. It seemed awkward, untoward, and utterly disconcerting.

"Of course," Daisy managed finally. She gestured, waving her hand around. "Where else would I stay? The marriage is just an arrangement."

To Daisy's dismay, she hiccupped. She winced, hoping her sister hadn't heard the graceless sound.

Lilly laughed. "I think you're in love with Mr. Honeycutt. Why don't you just admit it?"

"You're wrong!"

Lilly's amusement grew and she laughed again, shaking her head with disbelief over her sister's denial.

Daisy's dismay gave way to indignation. She hiccupped once more, stalked across the room and gave Lilly a small push out the door. "Why don't you keep your silly opinions to yourself, Lilly Muldoon?"

Lilly lifted her finger to her lips. "Shh. Kindly keep your voice down. I don't want you to wake my patient... you know, your *husband.*"

With a giggle, she darted away before Daisy could give her a piece of her mind. Lilly vanished into the shadows of the darkened hallway. A moment later, Daisy heard her sister's door close quietly. After that, the house was silent.

Chapter Thirty
Even the Weather is Better

Zach

Zach woke the next morning at sunrise. He lay in the narrow bed at the back of the cottage. Not the most comfortable bed, but a good bit better than the cot in the sawmill office.

He tucked his hands behind his head. A smile tugged at his lips. He, Zach Honeycutt, was married to a sweet, lovely, shy but tempestuous, young lady. He knew that marrying him hadn't been part of her plan, but he intended to change her mind, to show her it was meant to be.

He'd need a good strategy, one that involved her sisters. Poppy and Lilly were Daisy's weak spots. If he wanted to convince Daisy of anything, he'd have to take advantage of her weak spots. With that in mind, he considered how he might give her sisters what they most hoped for.

His plan for Lilly was easy and obvious. Lilly, the late bloomer, had a gift for nursing. She was diligent, caring and had a sharp mind. Lilly might not see that in herself, but he hoped that with time and opportunity, she'd come around.

Poppy, on the other hand, was a little more difficult. He'd like to think she'd be won over with a puppy. Maybe a kitten too, but he suspected that she might be the most stubborn of the three. He recalled how she'd cracked him across the head with the Trusty Mule. No, charming Poppy Muldoon might just prove to be the most difficult part of the puzzle.

He had to give the girl his grudging respect. She was shrewd and tenacious. He understood her better than she might guess.

After all, he too was the youngest of three siblings.

Before rising, he offered morning prayers. As the sun rose over the eastern horizon, he dressed quietly then slipped from the cottage. A short time later, he was on the road to the sawmill.

Halfway to the sawmill he realized he'd forgotten his coat. The cool morning air held a sharp chill, the last vestiges of winter. He shivered with the cold. No matter. Shoot, it could be sleeting, and he'd still feel content. He was married. To Daisy. He belonged to her, and she to him.

Sure, they had a heap of troubles to work around before they'd enjoy life together as man and wife, but they'd work them out together. Preferably back in Bethany Springs. A cool breeze stirred across the pines, prompting his horse to snort and prance.

As he neared the sawmill, the owner of a competing mill met him on the road. Mr. Jenkins had been by just a few days ago with an offer to buy the mill. Zach had refused.

"I'm ready to add ten percent to my offer," Mr. Jenkins said as he drew his horse alongside Zach's.

"That sounds promising."

"I hear talk around town. Things are looking better for your mill. You've only been there a few days, but production has increased from what I can see. Even the weather has improved. Men are talking about quitting their jobs and trying to hire on with your company because everyone says you're doing good things."

"The men probably heard I plan to shorten their day. Without lowering wages."

Mr. Jenkins grumbled. "Most mills push their men to produce more, not less."

"Tired men make mistakes. I've seen that time and again with my cowboys. Accidents happen at the end of cattle drives for the most part."

Mr. Jenkins shook his head with disbelief as if Zach was deliberately concealing some secret knowledge about sawmills.

Zach considered telling Mr. Jenkins how the Honeycutts always made sure their cowboys had good, solid horses, and a chance to not only get out of the saddle before sundown, but enjoy time for family, friends and worship.

"Would you at least consider my offer?" Jenkins asked impatiently.

"Yes, sir," Zach replied. He wanted to tell the man that any offer would have to get approval from the head of the family, but Mr. Jenkins looked like the type of man who might resent doing business with a woman.

Zach didn't bother mentioning that he'd spoken with two other owners of logging companies who were also eager to buy the mill. They were happy to offer top dollar. In truth, a sale suited Zach just fine. Pineville was pretty. The piney woods were special, but in his heart, he yearned to return to the big open skies of home, sooner rather than later, especially now that he had a wife.

He yearned to take Daisy to Bethany Springs, to show her the pretty hilltop overlooking the broad valley, the winding river threading through the stands of oaks, and share his dream of building a home on that very spot.

He hoped the day would come soon.

Chapter Thirty-One
Poppy Finds Another Treasure

Daisy

Daisy had hoped she'd wake up and discover that the past few weeks had all been a dream. That her Uncle Horace would still be alive, and that Mr. Honeycutt would not be real, and that she was not a married woman. It was ridiculous to hope for that, she knew, but the alternative was inconceivable.

Married? To Zachary Honeycutt?

She climbed out of bed and made her way to the back bedroom. She slowly opened the door and peered inside. The bed was empty, the blankets were in a heap, and Zach's coat was at the foot of the bed. It wasn't a dream.

Daisy fretted the entire morning. Zach had been a kindly, friendly gentleman up to now, but would he become a bossy, demanding husband? She'd seen how some husbands ordered their wives around.

He'd only asked for one thing: to let him take over searching for Horace's hidden stash of money. He made the request as they finished dinner the prior evening, their first dinner as man and wife.

You don't need to be prying up floorboards, Daisy. That's not a job for a young lady.

She hadn't missed the glint of humor in his eye when he talked about Horace's money. He probably thought the entire matter a fine joke, and why not? He'd never needed to fend for himself. He'd never gone without. Or scrimped. Or had to provide for younger siblings. Why would he care about an old man's life savings?

Horace's money was the one thing that could change matters. If she had the money, she could release Zach from his obligation, and she and her sisters could be on their way, maybe even to Biloxi. There, no one would know or need to know about Zachary Honeycutt or the strange turn of events from the past two days.

Despite Zach's request, Daisy felt compelled to continue her search. She reasoned that she could begin repairing the floor, since Zach had not told her otherwise, and in the process, if any attached floorboard happened to *accidentally* get caught by the end of the pry bar, that she'd go ahead and pull that board up, just to be sure it wasn't the one floorboard she'd been looking for.

She grabbed the pry bar and hammer and set about her task, but found her heart was not in it. A dull ache quickly set in. Her knees throbbed from the hard floor. She folded a blanket and knelt on the soft fabric but then her shoulders hurt, next her wrist.

When Lilly emerged from her room, still half asleep, she stopped in Horace's doorway. Daisy glanced up from her work. "I kept breakfast for you. It's on the stove."

"I thought Zach said he'd search for the money."

Daisy tapped the edge of the scuffed board with a small hammer, trying to coax it back between the neighboring planks. "I'm not looking for money."

Lilly yawned. "So, what are you doing?"

"I'm repairing the boards I pulled while I looked for the money. I don't want him working on this at the end of the day. Especially since his shoulder isn't entirely healed."

With the mention of Zach's injured shoulder, Lilly sprang to action. Daisy heard her eat a quick breakfast and rush back to her room to dress. A short while later, Lilly joined Daisy's efforts to repair the floorboards. They worked in companionable silence for the most part. As the morning passed, Poppy came into the room several times to comment on their progress or ask random questions.

Mostly, the young girl was bored. Without her sisters' attention, she amused herself with books or dressing Mrs. Cavendish in various outfits and hats that Uncle Horace had given her over the last few years.

Approaching midday, just as Daisy was about to fix some lunch, she heard a shriek from Poppy's room. She and Lilly stopped working, shared a concerned look and waited. The house was silent. Daisy wiped her brow and was about to tackle the next plank when Poppy hurried down the hall, flushed with excitement.

"I found something. A treasure!" she said breathlessly.

Daisy sighed. "That's wonderful. I'm sure you're hungry. Try to be patient."

"Don't you want to know what it is?"

"I do indeed. Tell me what you found. I can hardly wait to hear."

"Guess." Poppy whispered. "Guess what I found."

"We're busy," Lilly snapped. "Quit being a bother."

Poppy frowned at Lilly. When her sister ignored her, Poppy stuck out her lower lip and turned her attention to Daisy. She cradled her doll in her arms. "Mrs. Cavendish wants you to guess."

Daisy groaned inwardly. Anytime Poppy involved Mrs. Cavendish in a disagreement, Daisy would be required to converse with a doll, a doll that somehow took offense even more easily than Poppy. Worse, the arguments took twice as long. Still, there was no going back. Daisy proceeded to guess what Poppy might have found. After a half-dozen failed attempts, Daisy lost patience.

"I have no idea, Poppy. Sorry! I mean Mrs. Cavendish. And I'm not terribly interested, so can you just tell us please?"

Poppy lifted her chin. She crossed the room and sat on Horace's bed. She fluffed the pillow. With exaggerated deliberation, as if to make a point about feeling insulted, she laid Mrs. Cavendish on the pillow, arranging her arms and legs, straightening the doll's lace dress.

After Mrs. Cavendish had finally been comfortably settled, Poppy spoke. "Before I tell you what I found, you have to promise we'll go to Bethany Springs with Zach."

Daisy blinked, unsure what to say. "You want to go to see where Mr. Honeycutt lives?"

"I do. He promised to teach me to ride."

"He shouldn't make promises. I'm sorry to say that, Poppy, but we don't really know what will happen or what his intentions are."

Poppy wrinkled her nose. "Intentions?"

"His plans."

"You're wrong!" Poppy grew indignant. "The Honeycutts have an old horse that I can learn to ride, and Zach says he'll take all of us on picnics and that his mother loves children, and his family is big and loud and they love children too and we'd be more than welcome. That we'd have a home forever and ever."

Daisy's stomach clenched. "Poppy, listen-"

"And he says that he'll see about Lilly going to nursing school."

Lilly gave a slight nod. "He did."

"If you don't promise to go to Bethany Springs," Poppy shouted. "I won't tell you what I found. Something that belonged to Uncle Horace."

Poppy's voice echoed across the room. For a long moment, no one spoke. A memory flashed across Daisy's weary thoughts, a memory from only a few days before, a memory of Horace's gun and the moment she'd accidentally fired the small pistol.

"Tell me." Daisy's heart thudded. "*Please. Tell me that it's not another gun, is it?*"

"No." Poppy smiled triumphantly. "It's not a gun. It's better."

Daisy closed her eyes and let out a grateful sigh. She opened her eyes and nodded. "Go on."

"Promise we'll go to Bethany Springs with Zach."

"Fine, I promise."

Poppy's face lit with a joyous smile. She lifted her doll and flounced out of the room, promising to come right back. Daisy sat motionless, waiting. Lilly bent over her work, saying nothing as she studied the wood planks, pretending to choose the best match for the floor.

From the beginning, Daisy vowed not to give in to the heavy burden that came with her uncle's passing. She vowed, if only to herself, to rally, to pull herself together and protect her sisters. In her darkest moments, she meditated on a Bible quote her mother especially loved.

I can do all things through Him who strengthens me.

And with that, she prayed for help. And her prayers helped, they helped plenty, but still, she had doubts if she could carry the load.

Now that she and Zach were husband and wife, her sisters no longer needed her protection. Possibly. She knew Zach wanted to care for them, but that would require her to agree to this charade of marriage. It was like the load had been lifted off her shoulders and placed on her heart, and she wasn't sure she could manage.

Poppy dallied, somewhere in her room, talking to her doll as she rummaged through her things.

When she appeared in the hallway, she'd forgotten to bring Mrs. Cavendish. Her eyes shone with excitement. She carried a small bundle wrapped in damask.

Daisy stared, hardly daring to hope.

"Remember your promise," Poppy sang as she skipped into the room. Noting Daisy's expression, she came to a halt. "Remember?"

Daisy nodded. The sight of the small bundle sent a jolt down her spine. It shook her, crashing through her turmoil like a two-hundred-foot, prize East Texas pine. It seemed hardly possible. Had Poppy stumbled onto Horace's secret? Had the little girl found the money their family so desperately needed? Or the money they had once needed.

"Tell me you remember the promise," Poppy implored.

"I do." Daisy lifted her trembling hands, reaching for the bundle her sister cradled in her arms. "I remember."

Poppy laughed, a sweet, innocent sound of pure joy. She crossed the room and set the bundle in Daisy's outstretched hands.

The weight of the small parcel felt surprisingly light. She held it, considering its heft, or rather the lack. It was nothing compared to the bulk she'd dreamed of finding, less than the weight of one of her slim books, more than a measure of flour for a Sunday afternoon cake.

She hardly dared move and remained still, transfixed, kneeling on the hard, pine floor.

Quietly, Lilly came to her side and took the parcel. She slowly, wordlessly unwrapped the fabric.

Poppy was the first to make a sound, giggling, clapping and hopping from foot to foot as Lilly pulled back the final swath of fabric, revealing the money, a stack of bills bound by a short length of twine.

"It's Horace's money," Lilly said.

Chapter Thirty-Two
The Moonlight Garden

Zach

Zach's first day as a married man had been a glorious day, so far. He was aware that he wore a constant smile, but he couldn't change it. Several times he touched the side of his mouth and pulled down on the skin next to his lips, to force his face into a frown. Then he'd chuckle to himself and get back to his work. He'd never been so happy.

Then, the day changed.

The accident happened swiftly and without warning. A piece of lumber slipped from a saw, shot off the trestle and struck a young man. The impact knocked the fellow to the ground, where he lay for a good quarter of an hour. When he came to, he sat up and gazed around in bewilderment. Zach sent him home, accompanied by two other workers along with a week's pay.

"Tell his wife he's to stay in bed. I'm sending a week's wages with you. Give it to his wife. Tell her he's to stay home and get better, and that he's not to come to work or take any side jobs for the next week," Zach instructed.

For the rest of the afternoon, the workers had plenty to talk about. The mill boss had just announced shorter days with no change to wages, and now he'd paid a man to recuperate. They marveled at the notion, scarcely troubling with the details of the accident. Zach stayed later than usual to speak to various men about how to prevent another such accident.

The men listened with respect and agreed they could take more precautions regarding the saw, but several mentioned other accidents. The details turned his stomach. Normally, such things didn't bother him. Over the years, there'd been plenty of mishaps on the Honeycutt Ranch and at the family's silver mine, as well. Even Amelia had suffered a dislocated shoulder when she was thrown from a horse.

He rode home in the near darkness. A crescent moon glimmered through the thick pines. His thoughts wandered to the Muldoon girls. He wondered if Daisy had worried about him. Probably not. She kept herself busy. Feeling a tad sorry for himself, he imagined her going about her evening without so much as a passing thought about him.

After he tended to his horse, he went to the cottage. His heart skipped a beat as he drew near. He chastised himself for his romantic notions. For some reason, the accident that afternoon had left him feeling lonesome for Daisy. If only he could have her to himself. They'd talk about their day, perhaps even share a tender caress or heartfelt gaze.

As he neared the house, he spied a movement in the side yard. To his surprise, Daisy stood in the garden, studying a small bed of flowers. She hummed softly as she trailed her hand across the blooms. The breeze stirred, washing a delicate fragrance across the night air.

The sight of her in the dim moonlight struck his heart with a yearning he'd never known. He moved to the gate where he paused. The last thing he wanted was to startle her. Resting his hand on the latch, he cleared his throat.

"Hello there, Mrs. Honeycutt."

He wasn't sure what possessed him to use her married name. Perhaps to lay claim to her. Yes, that was it. He wanted to make the point that they were husband and wife despite the shaky beginnings of their marriage.

She drew a sharp breath. "Mr. Honeycutt."

He smiled inwardly. She'd turned his ploy back on him. Or that was how it seemed. On the other hand, she always called him Mr. Honeycutt.

He let himself into the garden. "All your flowers are white. Did you do that on purpose?"

"Yes," she replied softly. "It's a moonlight garden. My father used to plant one every year for my mother. Only his garden was ten times the size. It even had a small pond with evening blooming water lilies."

He circled the flower bed. To his dismay, Daisy edged away from him, keeping her distance. He frowned. Was she afraid of him? After the considerable time he'd stayed in the cottage, was it possible she feared him?

"A garden with a pond. Sounds romantic." His voice sounded gruff, even to his ear.

Daisy pursed her lips as she moved away from him again.

"Unless they ended up with a mess of mosquitos," he added, trying to make light of the topic. "Darned skeeters will wreck the most romantic evenings."

"You sound like an expert," she countered.

He chuckled, coming to a halt. He was enjoying their little back and forth, but he didn't care to chase her around the flower garden. Instead, he stood still and folded his arms. "Expert? I wouldn't go that far. That might be stretching things."

"You were engaged to be married," she said primly. "Have you written your fiancée to tell her you're married?"

209

"No. Not yet."

She paled. "You don't have a wife as well, do you?"

He laughed. "Just one. You, darlin'."

"When will you write her?" Daisy asked, her voice quiet.

"Soon as I can. I probably need to explain things to her parents. What's more, I need her address in England."

"She sounds fancy."

"Marie's fancy all right."

A look of pain flashed across Daisy's expression, so quickly he wondered if his eye played tricks on him. He rubbed the back of his neck and groaned softly. He hadn't imagined meeting Daisy in the garden like this, but he couldn't have imagined their meeting going this poorly.

He tried a new approach. "You know, Daisy. Us squabbling seems a real shame. Like a waste of a pretty moonlit evening." He tilted his head towards a low stone wall bordering the garden. "You and I are almost never alone. How about we sit together in the moonlight? Maybe I can even steal a kiss from my bride."

Her eyes shone in the silvery light as her face paled. She swallowed hard and looked away. He drew a weary sigh, wondering how he'd managed to make things worse.

Daisy gestured to the back door of the cottage. "I can give you supper. Lilly will want to examine your shoulder." He nodded and followed her inside. After Daisy brought him a plate, he gave thanks and ate even though he hardly tasted much of anything.

Daisy sat by a lamp and rummaged through her mending basket.

Poppy came to the table with her doll and wanted to know why he came late. Lilly sat by the fire, reading her medical volume. When he mentioned the accident, she came to the table wanting to know the details. She spoke of the different degrees of head injuries, based on what she knew. Zach assured her the young man would recover given time.

"I could visit the family," Lilly offered shyly. "I don't know very much but I'd be happy to help."

He shook his head. "I don't want you girls around the sawmill workers. They're a rough bunch."

Lilly nodded silently, looking disappointed. She brought her basket of bandages and dressing and began her regular evening task. She always looked so serious; Zach often had to keep from smiling. Sure, he'd had trouble with the wound, but Lilly approached the task with all the solemnity in the world.

She was always caring and kind but clearly viewed the work as the most important thing in her day. The wound was healing up just fine, but she liked to mother hen him and her two sisters. He unbuttoned the top few shirt buttons so she could rest assured he continued to heal.

"I've gotten my bell rung a time or two," Zach said as Lilly inspected his shoulder. "Just like the fella who got hurt today."

"You have?" Daisy asked, looking up from her mending.

"Probably why I'm so stubborn."

Lilly chuckled. Daisy turned back to work for a short time before excusing herself, murmuring a few words about needing to check on a matter.

When Daisy stepped out of the room, Lilly spoke in a low tone. "Did you and Daisy talk?"

Zach pushed his plate aside. "We talked all right."

Poppy and Lilly both leaned closer.

"Were you surprised?" Lilly asked.

Zach sighed. "Not really. But I don't want you to fret. I'll take care of things soon as I can."

She frowned with a hint of confusion but didn't ask for him to explain. She nodded, took her book from the nearby table, and wished Zach and Poppy a good night. "Don't stay up too late," she called.

"All right, Mother Hen," he grumbled, giving Poppy a wink.

Poppy eyed him with a broad smile and giggled. "Mother Hen. She is, isn't she? So bossy. Worse than Daisy even. Especially lately."

Before he could reply, Poppy asked Mrs. Cavendish what she thought. Zach waited, a smile tugging at his lips. After a moment, Poppy turned away from her doll, her expression solemn and thoughtful. "Mrs. Cavendish says they're both bossy and she's tired of their bossy ways."

Zach smiled and tugged Poppy's braid. "Tell Mrs. Cavendish that Lilly and Daisy boss folks around because they care."

Poppy wrinkled her nose, clearly not buying it. She bid him goodnight and left him alone in the empty room. He would have liked to talk more with Daisy, in hopes of ending the evening on a better note, but she didn't return. With a weary sigh, he rose from the table, washed his plate, and trudged down the long hallway to his room.

Chapter Thirty-Three
Amelia Gets Baffling News

Amelia

As she and Wade rode to Pineville, Amelia couldn't help feeling nostalgic. The piney woods reminded her of her childhood in Louisiana. The smell of the pine boughs and resin, the soft hush of wind as it moved through the treetops. Her senses reveled with long-forgotten memories.

She told Wade stories of long walks with her parents, exploring the majestic forests, a childhood lived amidst the endless stretch of trees. As much as she loved Bethany Springs, part of her heart would always remain in the Piney Woods.

Wade smiled and nodded, saying little as she shared her memories. Amelia noted a wave of warmth for Wade. She was grateful for his company.

As they approached Pineville, the road topped a crest. From this vantage point, she could see for a hundred miles or more. The small town of Pineville lay in the distance, a small, bustling enclave in the middle of a broad expanse of a deep forest green.

Since Amelia wasn't entirely sure where Zach's cabin was, she and Wade stopped at a large, busy store in the center of town, Cook's Mercantile.

"Would you like me to speak to the shopkeeper?" Wade asked, ever the gallant gentleman.

She was about to reply when, to her amusement, she noticed a rough patch of whiskers on his jaw. She suppressed a smile. It wouldn't do to make fun of Wade. At times he took offense easily.

They'd spent the prior night in a rustic boarding house in the middle of nowhere. The accommodations had not been to his liking. He'd grumbled about shaving with ice-cold water when they first set out on the road. He'd complained about the cold water for, oh, ten or twelve miles of their morning ride. She resolved not to mention the unshaven patch, for fear that he'd start complaining all over again.

"I'd like to take a look at the store without them knowing who I am."

His brows lifted with surprise.

"I want to get a feel for the town of Pineville."

"All right."

Wade and Amelia made their way into the store. Wade was immediately interested in a pair of hooked iron spikes that sat on a display. "What on earth?"

"They're for climbing trees. The loggers attach them to their boots so they can climb up a tree lickety-split."

"My word," he marveled.

"It keeps them from falling out of the tree."

He looked aghast as he hastily returned the irons to the display. "What a frightful prospect."

Amelia chuckled. "Really? I figured you'd want to hire on here. Work as a lumberjack."

"I'm afraid not. I haven't climbed a tree in several decades and I don't intend to start back now. Even if it meant working for my favorite sawmill owner."

She was about to respond when she spotted a lovely red-headed young lady enter the store with a young red-headed girl. They were clearly sisters, Amelia decided as they passed. The young lady nodded and with a sweet smile, bid them good morning.

Wade kept his attention fixed on the various tools on display.

Amelia found herself drawn to the girls and followed from a discreet distance. The younger girl fussed about a stick of candy. The older one chided her, refusing to listen to any talk about sweets. She spoke to the shopkeeper, asking for linens and bandages.

The shopkeeper smiled good-naturedly. "You mean to say that Zach is still ailing?"

Amelia drew a sharp breath. The girl turned to where Amelia stood a few paces away. Amelia lowered her gaze, pretending to study a jar of horse liniment. The girl turned back and spoke in a low voice.

Amelia shook her head with frustration. Well, this was aggravating. How was she supposed to eavesdrop when the girl spoke with such a cultured, demure tone? How did this lovely creature end up in such a rough town? And more importantly, why was she talking about Zach? Was it possible there was more than one Zach in Pineville?

She edged closer and held her breath, hoping to hear more, but the two girls wandered along the display counter, admiring the wares while the shopkeeper filled their order.

Just then Wade approached the counter. "Pardon me. Would you happen to be Mr. Cook? The proprietor?"

"No, Wade," Amelia whispered.

The shopkeeper stopped his task of unpacking a box of bandages and nodded. "I'm Mr. Cook."

"Excellent. I've come to Pineville with Mrs. Honeycutt."

215

Wade seemed to think his words would make an impact but probably not the response he received.

Mr. Cook froze, narrowing his eyes. The two girls turned slowly to stare at Wade.

Wade carried on, oblivious to his effect. He clasped his hands behind his back as if addressing a judge or jury. "More importantly, do you happen to know where the supervisor's cabin is?"

"Why you want to know that?" Mr. Cook asked, his tone edged with a subtle air of threat.

The conversation wasn't off to a good start. Amelia guessed it would only go downhill from that point and strode to the counter. "I'm Mrs. Honeycutt."

Mr. Cook narrowed his eyes with unmistakable doubt. The older of the two girls gasped softly.

The younger girl rushed to Amelia's side, her eyes blazing with fury. "You're not Mrs. Honeycutt," she insisted, her face reddening. "My *sister* is Mrs. Honeycutt."

The older girl walked down the length of the aisle with slow measured steps. She stared at Amelia. Something in her gaze spoke of recognition. The silence stretched between them until the girl slowly set her hand on Amelia's arm.

"You're Zach's mother."

"I am. And you are?"

The girl frowned as she considered the question. She winced and appeared awkward as she mulled over her answer. "I suppose I'm his sister-in-law."

The younger girl looked affronted. "What am I?"

"You're a sister-in-law too," the older girl said.

The girl's lips curved into a happy smile. "Oh! That's nice."

Amelia's thoughts swirled. Her mind refused to believe what she had heard. Suddenly, her knees felt wobbly. She gave a slight murmur of distress.

Wade came to her side, quickly wrapping an arm around her shoulders and drawing her to a nearby chair. He spoke soothingly as Amelia's thoughts whirred like spinning tops. Zach married? It wasn't possible.

It couldn't be so. After all, Zach was engaged to Marie.

Chapter Thirty-Four
The Oxcart Tips

Daisy

Daisy had intended to shop at the mercantile that morning, but after a restless night, she woke, determined to speak to Zach. She'd tell him about finding Horace's money and how she hoped to take her sisters to live somewhere else. Anywhere that wasn't Pineville. Why hadn't she given her plan more thought? She chided herself for not planning her next step.

She went to the sawmill, but one of his men explained that he'd gone to the logging site and wasn't expected back till later. The news gave her pause. Uncle Horace didn't approve of her spending time amongst the loggers, and Zach vehemently disapproved of the matter. She recalled how he'd insisted she stop selling lunches to the men.

She couldn't wait to speak to Zach, however. Not after she'd found the money and especially not after he'd spoken of kissing her in the moonlight. She'd speak to him now, return to the cottage and make arrangements to leave Pineville. Perhaps Zach would be willing to look into an annulment. The thought made her eyes sting, but she forged on, making her way up the road to the logging site, driven by the need to set things straight.

As she drew closer, she scanned the area for a sign of Zach. Oxcarts, loaded with freshly cut logs, rumbled past, heading to the sawmill. The drum of axes echoed around her. Every so often one of the loggers would shout, alerting his neighbors of the falling tree. *Timber*!

The word was often greeted with a cheer or perhaps a good-natured ribbing. The men worked as teams but that didn't mean they didn't enjoy taunting each other about the rate of falling trees. Or perhaps that was the reason.

They all regarded her with surprise. A few shouted to ask if she brought lunch, but she waved off their questions. With a smile, they offered gestures of exaggerated disappointment before waving and returning to work.

Suddenly, Zach appeared from the thick growth of pine. His eyes flashed with disapproval. He stalked out from the forest shadows, meeting her at the bend of the road.

"You shouldn't be here." His gruff voice startled her. For a moment she wondered if she would have the will to speak frankly.

"I need to talk to you."

"Here?"

She nodded.

"Is something wrong? Is someone ill or hurt?"

"No."

"Then it can wait until this evening. If you don't want to talk in front of your sisters, we'll talk in the garden."

The garden. The mere mention of the garden sent a wave of indignation through her. In an instant, she gathered her scattered thoughts. She needed to speak to him here and now. It couldn't wait.

"I found Horace's money," she said.

His expression softened. Barely. Enough to give her a small push to continue. "It's not a lot but it's enough for my family to leave Pineville and find a home someplace else."

For a long moment, he didn't reply. Instead, he tugged off his leather gloves, clasped them in one hand and folded his arms across his chest. For some reason, the gesture made him look bigger and broader than usual. It didn't help that he'd narrowed his eyes and looked decidedly irritated.

"Your family?" he asked quietly. "*Your* family?"

"Yes." She frowned, wondering why he'd ask for clarification.

"All right." He nodded, let his gaze drift off for a moment before returning to her. "So where are we going?"

"We?"

"Yes. We, Daisy, because I am part of your family, and you are part of mine."

She swallowed hard. He wasn't making this easy on her. In some part of her heart, she'd imagined Zach hadn't been sincere about being man and wife. Or that he went along with the vows as an act of charity. She'd expected that he might be relieved to hear she and her sisters would be leaving Pineville. He looked anything but pleased.

"You have your own life, Mr. Honeycutt."

"Stop calling me that," he said from between gritted teeth.

Lifting her chin, she went on. "It's true, *Zach*. You have your own life, complete with a girl who expects to marry you. I have to care for my sisters which means I can't get distracted by a man offering to kiss me in the moonlight."

"We're married, Daisy. I'm real clear on your lack of fondness for moonlight kisses, but if you're leaving Pineville, I'll be the one taking you. And that's that."

She recoiled. "You can't make me stay. I can leave if I want to."

He shrugged a shoulder. "If you leave, I promise I'll find you."

Staring at him, she tried to make sense of his words. He claimed that he'd find her if she left. Did he intend to track her down?

"You might not care for kissing, but I'm still your husband. Which means I take care of you. No way will I let you hightail it from Pineville with your pitiful little bit of savings and fend for yourself. I agree you shouldn't be here. It's not safe. But I will provide for you and your sisters. I'm your husband. I will be the one to take you to a better place."

His words astonished her, leaving her without an immediate reply. The entire conversation had gone so far afield, and she wasn't sure why or how. One thing for certain, she'd made absolutely no headway by coming to speak to him.

"I should go home," she said.

"I'll take you."

She shook her head. Before she could argue, one of the loggers called for Mr. Honeycutt. There was a quarrel between two logging teams. The men were ready to brawl.

Zach muttered under his breath.

"I can walk alone," Daisy said. "I'm used to it."

Angry shouts came from the trees along the rise.

With a quick word of farewell, Daisy turned and began the trip home. Her mind spun with turmoil. She hadn't expected Zach's response. He'd been so insistent on his role of provider and protector. Emotions swirled inside her. On one hand, she couldn't help feeling pleased and flattered. On the other hand, she wondered if Zach Honeycutt might be the type of man who relished his power a little too much. What if he was a tyrant?

She'd never dealt with such a mass of conflicting feelings.

A wagon rumbled down the road behind her. She moved out of the way. As the wagon neared, it lurched to one side and at the same instant a crack rent the air. The logs toppled. Daisy tried to jump out of the way but tripped over a deep rut. A giant log rolled towards her. Before she could flee its path, the thicker span crashed into a nearby tree. The top, narrow part rolled on top of her ankle, knocking her down, pinning her to the hard road.

Pain stole her breath. Shock squeezed her throat. She tried to cry for help. No sound came from her lips. She fell back, her head hitting the ground. Agony shot the length of her body. Trying simply to draw breath, she stared up at the sky. The pines soared above her, reaching for a small spot of blue sky. She wanted to call for Zach but couldn't summon the strength. Zach. She yearned for him to come, more than she'd ever could have imagined. Her sight grew dim and faded to darkness.

Chapter thirty-five
News of Daisy's Accident

Amelia

Lilly Muldoon invited Amelia and Wade to the family cottage. She explained it was only fitting since they were practically family. Amelia had been too astonished to accept the invitation, but Wade had no such trouble.

The cottage belonged to the sawmill and was a rough-hewn structure that had been added onto over the years. The interior was tidy and well-kept. The furnishings were slightly tattered, but respectable. Lilly invited them to sit in the sun-filled parlor. She hurried to the kitchen to fix some refreshments, leaving the younger girl with Wade and Amelia.

Poppy was a talkative child. She chattered on about everything except for what Amelia most wished to know. How did Zach end up married to the eldest of the three Muldoon girls?

Amelia half listened to the child prattle on. Wade did a fine job pretending to be interested, asking this and that. The girl showed him her doll. Meanwhile, the older girl wreaked havoc in the kitchen. In the space of five minutes, she managed to break three dishes. Amelia left Wade to fend for himself and wandered to the kitchen door.

"Everything all right?" she asked.

Lilly brushed a lock of hair from her eyes as she swept up ceramic shards. "I wish Daisy were here. She's a better hostess."

"Thank you for your hospitality," Amelia offered in a soothing tone. "Neither you nor your sister expected company. It's mighty nice of you to invite us in."

"It's not like her to leave without leaving a note. I can't imagine where she is."

"It's fine, Lilly. Please don't fret on our account." Amelia spoke in a calm voice that belied her inner turmoil. She drifted to the window, tugged back the curtain, and gazed out to the side yard. The garden was filled with a profusion of colorful flowers from patches of well-tended beds to pots along the walkway, brimming with vibrant blooms. Amelia felt herself smile despite her worries.

She let out a weary sigh, trying to imagine how she came to find herself in this position.

Zach had married a stranger. Not ten days ago he'd proposed to poor, sweet Marie. Amelia's heart felt heavy as she tried to imagine explaining the situation to Sophie. Her dear friend would be heartbroken. Amelia felt her own heart ache even though she knew Zach wouldn't commit to marriage unless he was absolutely sure.

Letting the curtain fall back, she turned away from the pretty garden.

Lilly made tea. She set cups, saucers, and a plate of cookies on a tray. Amelia noted the girl's trembling hands and came to her side to help. When the tray was ready, Amelia gently shooed the girl aside and carried it to the parlor where Wade chatted, not only with the youngest Muldoon sister but also with the doll.

Amelia felt her lips tug to a reluctant smile.

"I *do* like campfires, Mrs. Cavendish," Wade said, his expression earnest. "I like them just fine. Especially when I'm visiting Bethany Springs."

The girl beamed. With the doll perched on her knee, she playacted more questions for Wade. "What about oatmeal cookies? Do you like them?"

"I like them too," Wade answered as he gave Amelia a wink.

"With raisins or without?" Poppy demanded in a croaking voice.

"Oh, Poppy, don't bother the nice man," Lilly fussed.

Wade waved off Lilly's concerns and kept up the lively conversation. "I have strong feelings on cookies, Mrs. Cavendish. I must confess that I like any kind of cookie. I'm not at all particular if they have raisins or if they don't have raisins."

Poppy eyed him with no small degree of suspicion. Clearly, she didn't entirely approve of Wade's response. Amelia wondered what answer the girl would find acceptable. Many people had strong feelings about such notions. Raisins? Or no raisins? The subject was a serious one, especially for some folks, just like the topic of beans in chili, an issue that could lead to a heated debate amongst her own three boys.

Lilly fidgeted in a nearby chair, looking paler by the moment. Amelia couldn't help feeling a little sorry for the girl. She offered a gentle smile as she took it upon herself to serve the refreshments. She poured a cup of tea for Wade, herself, and Lilly. She didn't offer Poppy any tea since the child seemed content to question Wade on the subject of raisins.

Lilly shushed her sister. Poppy stuck out her lower lip but didn't argue. Lilly fixed her gaze on Amelia and began to tell the girls' story.

"We had intended to leave Pinewood after Uncle Horace passed away," Lilly said, her voice shaking. "But we needed to find the money he'd hidden. He always said he was saving up to do something special for the three of us. He worried about getting robbed since logging sites often invited rough types. Uncle Horace always felt safer stashing valuables under the floorboards, you see."

"Of course," Wade said. "Makes perfect sense."

Amelia arched a brow. Wade was always polite and eager to ease people's distress. She watched as he blew on his cup of tea, pretending to be a fellow who drank hot tea all the time instead of heavily sweetened iced tea.

"Go on," Amelia said gently.

"The problem was, he never told us where exactly he hid his valuables."

Amelia winced. That sounded just like a man. He probably decided to protect his girls by hiding the money but didn't quite trust females enough to explain *where* he'd hidden the valuables.

Lilly went on to explain the story of Zach coming to Pinewood and learning of their predicament. He'd directed the girls to stay put, that he'd sleep in the sawmill office. He'd give them time to find their uncle's money. He still dropped by to check on them out a sense of concern. During one of the visits, a gun was discovered by Poppy. It was small but loaded. When Daisy grabbed it, she accidentally fired the gun.

Nobody spoke. Quiet filled the small drawing room. Amelia felt her heart pound in her chest.

Lilly paused and bit her lip. "She shot Zach in the shoulder."

Amelia nodded, hardly daring to breathe.

"He's fine," Poppy exclaimed. "Lilly fixed his sore shoulder."

"Isn't that something?" Wade murmured as he set his cup down. He winced as he directed his gaze to Lilly. "Hard to imagine you tended to that sort of wound. A bullet? Why, you're just a girl."

"I did my best." Lilly clasped her hands tightly. "My uncle had a big book of various treatments. Ever since I found it, I've read as much as I could."

"I'm grateful," Amelia said quietly.

"I was happy to do it." She lowered her gaze for a long moment before going on. "Zach told me that he could help me attend a school in Galveston. So I could learn how to be a nurse."

Amelia spoke. "That might be possible."

The younger girl brightened. "He told me that he'd show me how to ride."

Amelia smiled. "Did he now?"

"So, about their marriage." Lilly pressed her lips together. After a long moment, she went on. "The townsfolk heard of him staying here. They came and insisted Zach and Daisy marry. They agreed and said their vows right there on the porch."

"Oh, my," Wade said, shaking his head with surprise.

Lilly went on. "That was two days ago. Daisy and Zach aren't really..."

Amelia nodded, understanding what Lilly meant. She glanced at Poppy who appeared preoccupied with her doll's hair ribbons.

Amelia finished Lilly's thought, choosing her words carefully. "It's just an arrangement for the time being. Given how quickly things happened."

"Yes, ma'am. I don't think Daisy really believes Zach will follow through with the arrangement."

"What do you mean by that?" Amelia asked, more sharply than she'd intended.

Lilly didn't avert her eyes. Instead, she forged on, her voice shaking a little more than before. "Daisy told me he's engaged to be married."

Before Amelia could respond, Wade shook his head. "Zach's engaged, but he agreed to the engagement purely out of friendship."

"What on earth do you mean?" Amelia wasn't entirely surprised by Wade's comment but wondered how he knew about the matter while she hadn't heard anything.

He shrugged and looked sheepish.

"They never intended to marry?" Amelia demanded.

"Marie told me before she left. She begged me not to tell her father or mother, that they'd never allow her to travel if she wasn't engaged to Zach."

Amelia's thoughts swirled. She wasn't sure if she ought to feel furious or amused by the entire matter. One thing was certain, she knew that Sophie would be angry and embarrassed and worried about Marie traveling with her young daughter. She let out a long, weary sigh. She had to imagine how much Zach had fretted about his predicament.

Zach's hasty marriage could stir up plenty of bad feelings between the Honeycutts and the McCords. Despite that, Amelia had no doubt her son had done the honorable thing.

She and Wade shared a look, and she knew he was thinking the very same thing. A surge of warmth wrapped around her heart. Wade was a kind soul, she had to admit, and she also had to admit that she felt a deep sense of gratitude that he'd revealed Marie's secret even if it would cost him dearly when they eventually returned to Bethany Springs.

A wagon rumbled down the road. Amelia heard the driver shout to the animals to stop. The wagon slowed, came to a halt and footsteps pounded up the pathway. Amelia listened to the sound. The footfalls sent a shudder along her spine as if she knew somehow the person bore some fearful message. Her memory shot back in time to when she was a young wife with two boys and a child on the way. She'd received the news of George's passing in much the same way. And yet, somehow, she knew this news wasn't for her. She turned her gaze to Lilly, who seemed to know the message was for her family.

Wade took charge. He directed the women to stay put. Amelia reached across the table and took Lilly's hand in hers as they listened to Wade speak to the messenger. The man spoke with a heavy Spanish accent, trying this best to explain why he'd come.

It took some time for Wade to calm the man. He even managed a few words in Spanish, to Amelia's surprise. Wade stumbled around with various phrases that may or may not have been of help. Finally, the man drew a deep sigh and said a few words of prayer asking for the good Lord's help before he spoke the words he'd come to say.

Amelia gripped Lilly's hand. If she'd felt sorry for the girl earlier, she only felt more so now. It seemed the girl had expected some calamity and now she looked as if she might wilt from the afternoon's events. Amelia held her hand tightly, but Lilly's grip was at least twice as firm.

Both Lilly and Amelia sat quietly. Keeping their gazes averted, they waited to hear what the news would bring.

The man spoke haltingly.

There'd been an accident. Mrs. Honeycutt was hurt. Her husband took her to Jasper Grove, thirty miles away...

He coughed and took a moment to compose himself. Wade urged him to finish. After a brief pause, the man went on.

The town has a hospital. Built only two months ago. It was closer than the other hospital. New. Close. They could help. All would be well. God willing...

Chapter thirty-Six
That One is Called Devotion

Daisy

Daisy's dreams and memories swirled in her mind. They were like two sides of a family who lived on opposite sides of the world, never visiting each other, normally. Now, they danced together, and played together, an odd assortment of visions and feelings that both confused and delighted Daisy. She heard her own mind ask, *Is this real?* And just as quickly, she joined in the experience again, fascinated and stricken by the world in her mind.

A jolt of pain shot through her, or so it seemed. Just as quickly it was gone again. She started to roll over in her sleep, and the oxcart flashed back into memory. Instantly, she was awake.

The pain of the log hitting her ankle was vivid in her mind. She'd prayed for Zach to come. She could picture the moment he came to her side, lifted the immense limb from her leg. And then he'd lifted her gently, promising that he'd take care of everything.

Zach wrapped her in a blanket before he set her on the bed of the wagon, her hurt leg on a soft bed made from the men's coats. She recalled one man taking off his coat and laying it on the wagon bed. By the time Zach set her down, many more men had added their coats to the pile, building a small bed for her leg.

The ride on the buckboard had been hard, each bump in the road feeling like a new injury. Without the coats, she would have fainted from the pain, she was sure of that. Amidst the hard memories, she remembered the way Zach held her hand and spoke soothingly for the entire journey.

She faded back to sleep.

She awoke and found herself in a hospital room, her ankle wrapped in a thick bandage, her entire leg held in a brace suspended from a rod above her bed. The first rays of sunshine glowed through the curtains; soft hues of coral edged with gold. Sunrise.

How long had she been there at the hospital? There was no way to tell. A noise drew her attention. On the right-hand side of her bed, she found Zach fast asleep. He lay slumped over, resting his head on his arms. He dozed, snoring softly.

She drew a sharp breath and reached to the tousled mop of hair, wishing to brush the stray locks from his brow, but stopped herself. Why wake him? He rested peacefully. She ought to let him sleep a little longer. Noting his unshaven jaw, she wondered if he'd been by her side for some time. Her heart warmed as she let her gaze drift over his features.

Zach. Her Zach. He'd stayed. For how long, she didn't know. She shouldn't feel pleased he was there by her side, but she could hardly help herself. A smile tugged her lips.

The door opened. Lilly appeared with a parcel in her arms.

"Lilly," Daisy said softly.

"You're awake! I was so worried about you."

Lilly hurried to Daisy's side and squeezed her hand. Daisy felt her sister's touch through her arm and into her heart. A tear streamed down her cheek.

"I come bearing gifts."

"What did you bring?"

Her sister smiled as she rounded the foot of the bed. "Sorry. Nothing for you. I brought clean clothes for Zach. His mother sent them to my room this morning. She said it was time the man bathed and changed. He was beginning to smell a tad rank."

Daisy glanced at Zach and then back to Lilly. "How long has he been here?"

"Three days."

Daisy blinked. Her gaze drifted from Lilly to Zach and back again. "Three days?"

Lilly nodded.

"No. It's not possible. I can't recall any of that time."

Lilly set the parcel on the bedside table. "It's true. A day or two of sleep after a trauma is normal, but three days! We were all really worried, but none as much as Zach. He refused to leave."

Daisy heard her sister's words but found it difficult to take in the significance. Zach had stayed by her side for three days. How was it possible? To her thinking, it was more likely that Lilly would remain by her side. Her loyal, dutiful sister would be the one to keep vigil.

"Did you stay with him?" Daisy asked quietly.

Lilly paled and shook her head. "No, I'm sorry. I couldn't bear it."

Daisy waited for more of an explanation.

Lilly went on. "I'm not sure if I'm meant to be a nurse. I ought to just work in a mercantile or a dress shop."

"What?"

Her sister looked resolute. "I nearly passed out when I saw that you were in so much pain. I think I felt it right along with you, maybe even worse. I felt completely helpless. If I can't tolerate seeing someone in pain, I have no business as a nurse. It's not my calling."

Daisy sighed. "Lilly."

Her sister clasped her hand. "Yes."

"Just hush, would you?"

Lilly rolled her eyes and set Daisy's hand aside. Zach stirred. Lilly leaned down to kiss Daisy on her brow. She excused herself, went to the door and promised to return later that evening.

"Where are you staying?" Daisy asked. A flutter of worried thoughts sent her mind into a familiar swirl of concern. She'd been in charge of her sisters' well-being for so long, she couldn't imagine how they'd fare without her.

"We're in the hotel. Mrs. Honeycutt paid for three whole rooms! It's very nice. She and Poppy have become fast friends."

Lilly waved her fingers and slipped from the room. Hardly a moment later, Zach roused from sleep. He groaned and rubbed the back of his neck as he got to his feet and let out a weary sigh. Stopping at the foot of the bed, he eyed her with surprise.

"Sweetheart," he said, his voice rough from sleep. He gazed at her as a slow smile curved his lips. "You're awake."

Zach looked really rough, like he'd been lost in the forest for a few days. His shirt was rumpled, his hair disheveled. A short beard darkened his jaw. She couldn't resist an answering smile.

"I am. Have I been sleeping a great deal?"

He shrugged a shoulder, keeping his gaze fixed on her. He continued to smile at her, clearly pleased she'd finally woken. The sweet, endearing expression did something funny to her heart, making it flutter unexpectedly.

"Well," she prompted. "Did I sleep for days?"

He nodded. "You needed your rest. You woke here and there. I helped you with a few meals, but you tired easily. The good news is that the doctor said I could take you outside today."

"Outside?" she glanced at her bandaged foot. It didn't hurt but she'd assumed that was because she hadn't moved. She could hardly think about what had happened or her injury. Dread coiled around her heart. What if she'd been crippled or left with a lifelong limp?

Zach unwrapped the parcel Lilly had brought. He briefly inspected the contents before pouring water into a basin. He began to strip out of his shirt as he spoke casually of her surgery and the doctor's instructions.

"Doc says you'll be in pain for a few weeks, but it should subside by and by." He grumbled under his breath, something about how badly he needed a shave.

Daisy tried to ignore her husband as he soaped and splashed water.

"Dang, that water was mighty cold," he muttered as he dried off. A moment later, he buttoned a fresh shirt, and carried on with his talk of the events of the past few days.

Daisy listened as she summoned the courage to wriggle her toes. She winced, expecting the worst. She wriggled. Slightly at first and then a little more vigorously. To her surprise, she hardly noted any pain, just a slight discomfort. She felt encouraged. Still, she couldn't imagine setting weight on her foot. The pain from that effort might prove too much.

Zach went on about the food in the hospital. He said it wasn't fit to feed a mule. He complained about the night nurse who he suspected didn't like him one bit at first but had come around after their first meeting when he'd demanded clean linens for her bed.

"You'd think I asked for the moon," he grumbled coming to her bedside. "All I wanted was some clean bedsheets for my wife. Are you ready?"

She recoiled. "For what?"

He held out his hands. "For me to carry you outside. Your room has a private garden. I'm going to take you to the sitting area."

"C-carry me?" She tugged the bedsheet to her chin and regarded him with alarm. "I don't believe I care to venture outside."

"Well, that's a darned shame. The doc says that starting today, you need to visit the garden twice a day. The sunshine will do you good."

"I'm not dressed. Or not properly."

"You're in a sleeping gown. Won't matter. No one can see you but me." His eyes flashed mischievously.

Her door opened and a nurse came in. Zach moved over and the nurse deftly unhooked her leg and gently lowered it to the bed so she could help Daisy wash her face, brush her teeth, and fix her hair. Just as quickly the nurse left again.

Zach lowered his voice to a conspiratorial whisper. "If you're worried about propriety, I'm your husband now. And I've been with you since the accident. I've seen plenty, Mrs. Honeycutt."

She drew a sharp breath. "What is that supposed to mean?"

"I'll tell you some other time," he said playfully.

"Oh, goodness."

"Quit your grousing, Daisy. You've only been awake a few minutes and you've been grumbling the whole time."

Before she could argue the point, he proceeded with his plan. He snatched a pillow, tucked it under his elbow, scooped her in his arms, and strode to the door leading to the garden. The door was ajar, so he nudged it open with the toe of his boot. It swung wide. He smiled down at her before carrying her from the shadowed hospital room and into the bright, warm sunshine.

After days of sleep and resting indoors, the dazzling sunlight made her eyes water. She looped her arm around his neck, squeezed her eyes shut and pressed her forehead to his shoulder.

"What if..." her words trailed off.

"What if what?"

"What if I can't walk?"

"You will."

She felt his pace slow and then come to a stop. Without lifting her head or opening her eyes, she went on. "What if it takes a long time for me to walk again?"

"Then I'll carry you. I'll take you anywhere you need to go."

His reply came at once and without reservation. His gentle tone brought a lump to her throat. When he pressed a kiss to her head, her eyes stung with tears. His devotion overwhelmed her. It was all too much for her to take in.

"Daisy," he said quietly. "I can see you're still fretting. My mother has a favorite Bible quote. From the book of Luke. *Who of you by worrying can add a single hour to your life?*"

Slowly, she lifted her head and looked into his eyes. In the past she'd wondered if he was sincere in the things that he told her. Was he speaking truthfully? Or was he merely toying with her heart? Now she clearly saw the warmth in his eyes. She knew without a doubt that he spoke from his heart. She cupped his jaw with her hand and stroked her thumb across his face.

"Don't worry, Daisy. Take a little time to heal. Let yourself take a break from working so hard to care for everyone. You're always tending to other people, like your sisters for example, or me. For once, let someone take care of you."

His words stole her breath and left her speechless. She nodded. He smiled, kissed her forehead, and set her down on the wrought-iron bench. He set the small pillow he'd carried, under her heel with such tenderness she was left astonished.

"Hurts?" he asked.

"No. Not at all."

With a shy smile, he sat beside her and took her hand in his. The warmth sent an agreeable shiver along her skin. His hand felt both strong and gentle. His rough palm suggested the long hours of hard work he did each day. The tender touch made her think of his gruff but kind heart. He eyed the garden thoughtfully and began pointing out the flowers in the surrounding beds, asking what they were called.

Daisy allowed herself to enjoy the sweet moments with Zach, reminding herself that worrying wouldn't make things better. Zach was devoted to her. She understood that now. She could see that he had every intention of fulfilling his vows. The realization made her heart warm in ways she'd never known, and she could imagine a future with this man, a future they'd both enjoy when she was healed.

She set her fears aside and let the spring sunshine warm her. She spoke of the various blooms, telling Zach about each flower. He listened, a smile playing upon his lips as he held her hand clasped firmly in his.

"Daisy," he said quietly. "What would you think if I stole a kiss? Right here in this little garden."

She smiled. "It's not stealing if I agree to the kiss."

Gently, he cupped her jaw and lowered to kiss her lips. His tender touch warmed her heart. From that moment on, Daisy and Zach shared more kisses. Daisy was sure that each one was even sweeter than before.

Chapter thirty-Seven
Not the Picnic He'd Imagined

Zach

A month had passed since the night they exchanged vows on the porch of the Pineville cottage. Since that night, a great deal had happened, starting with the accident in the woods, followed by Daisy's stay at the hospital. He'd remained by her side for the entire hospital stay, refusing to leave.

As her leg healed, he cared for her and along the way did what he could to prove his love. It seemed to him that somehow the cart had ended up before the horse. The wedding and the courting were backwards. Courting before vows. He was determined to fix things. Pronto.

At first, Daisy seemed to be skeptical about their marriage. He was sure she figured he wasn't sincere when he tried to tell her how devoted he was. How many times did he need to explain? She belonged to him. He belonged to her. Forever.

She'd done her best to resist him as he stayed by her bedside. She continued to keep him at arm's length. Things changed, however, when he took her home to Bethany Springs. He recalled the exact moment when Daisy finally believed.

Poppy and Lilly were already in Bethany Springs, staying with Mama in the big house. He drove up to the house and halted the wagon. The two girls heard their arrival and flew out the door. Mama hurried a few paces behind.

The girls bounded down the steps and rushed to the buckboard to greet Daisy. In that moment, Daisy's eyes shone with emotion. Her shoulders shook. After she greeted her sisters, she regarded him with surprise. Till then she hadn't allowed herself to believe they were truly married, truly a family till she'd seen her sisters there on Mama's porch.

Now, he'd like to say he'd won her over. She'd stopped calling him Mr. Honeycutt and called him Zach, or beefcake, or some other endearment related to his size and strength. While Lilly and Poppy stayed with Mama in the big house, he and Daisy had taken a small, nearby cabin until their home could be built.

His sister-in-law, Lilly, liked to offer pointers on how best to court her stubborn sister. Most of the time she had her nose in a book, studying for her nursing school exam. Other times, she seemed to enjoy poking fun at his romantic attempts. She'd sigh and act like he was a lost cause when it came to romantic notions and told him as much.

Precisely one month after the wedding, Lilly had a suggestion for Zach.

"You ought to do something romantic for your anniversary," Lilly said.

"Who are you talking to?" Zach asked.

"You, Zach. Today is May seventh. You've been married exactly one month."

Mama set her coffee mug down and nodded, giving him a pointed look. "That's a fine idea."

Zach wanted to argue that he had a dozen romantic plans in store for their anniversary. Truth was, he didn't. He was head over heels in love with Daisy, the happiest man alive, but maybe not the smartest. Should he have known that thirty days constituted an anniversary? He hadn't considered that, and he wasn't sure how to proceed. If he'd only had one good, romantic idea, he'd take Lilly on in a friendly argument, but he couldn't come up with even one.

Somehow his mother understood the guilty look on his face. Of course, she did. Mama turned to Daisy and patted her hand, giving her a look of sympathy.

Daisy couldn't hold back a soft laugh.

Zach tried to salvage matters. Grumbling under his breath, he helped himself to a few more slices of bacon. "I'm plenty romantic."

Poppy sat across the table from Daisy and gestured to where her doll sat in the chair beside her. "Mrs. Cavendish loves romantic things."

Zach didn't reply. He understood the lay of the land. As the only male at the table, he was outnumbered. Mama, Lilly and Poppy eyed him with expectation. Even Mrs. Cavendish seemed to be giving him the side eye. He turned to find his sweet bride smiling with a teasing glint in her eye.

His well-planned defense slipped from his thoughts. One look at Daisy made his thoughts fall into disarray. He couldn't help himself.

Daisy. His sweet Daisy.

He considered leaning close to whisper a few romantic things in her ear. She'd certainly found them charming and utterly romantic the last few nights.

Instead of helping him in his moment of need, she drew back, her smile widening as she left him to fend for himself.

He held his tongue. Instead of arguing, he made a note to set aside the work he'd intended to do that day. He knew right there that his day wouldn't include fence repair, or branding the yearlings, nor halter training the new foals. Not today. Today he was taking his bride for a picnic.

As far as the chores that awaited him? Well, it was clear. The decision was made. He'd have to assign the tasks to his ranch hands.

He leaned and took Daisy's hand in his, then brushed a kiss across the top. "What about a romantic picnic, Mrs. Honeycutt? We can take a basket and enjoy lunch on the spot where we'll build our house."

He imagined having her all to himself, sitting on the hilltop and sharing their dreams. A rush of warmth came over him. A romantic picnic for their one-month anniversary. He'd already shown her the spot where they'd build their home. Now he relished the notion of going back. It would give them a chance to talk more of their plans and their dreams. He'd hold her in his arms and tell her how much she meant to him. Why hadn't he thought of it himself?

"That would be lovely," Daisy said shyly.

Zach drew a deep, contented breath.

Mama chuckled. "I'll make some sandwiches. Poppy can help me make a peach pie."

Zach winced. Was Mama planning to come? And Poppy too? His idea of a romantic picnic involved two people, not the whole family.

Lilly chimed in. "I'll help make the sweet tea and pack the basket."

"What now?" he asked.

Lilly frowned. "Unless you want lemonade instead of tea."

"I like both," Poppy offered. "I believe Mrs. Cavendish does too."

"The three of you are coming along?" Zach asked. "For a romantic picnic?"

"Yes," Poppy replied with a knit brow. "Don't forget Mrs. Cavendish. She's coming too. That makes four of us coming along for your romantic picnic."

Daisy laughed softly as she set her hand on his arm. "A picnic sounds very nice. I'd like that very much."

Zach agreed to the plan. He would have preferred to go alone with Daisy to their hillside picnic overlooking the river, but his wife's sweet smile made him forget any of his own preferences. Whenever Daisy smiled at him, Zach only wanted what she wanted.

He lifted her hand to brush a kiss across the top. Softly, he whispered, "I love you, Daisy. Fact is, I love you more every day."

She blushed. "And I love you too, Zach, with all my heart."

Epilogue
Summer on Galveston Island

Amelia

After two solid months of study, Lilly Muldoon braved the nursing school entrance exams. Amelia felt sorry for the poor girl. Ever since Lilly decided to apply, she'd been a nervous wreck. Amelia tried her best to encourage Lilly, but to no avail. Daisy and Zach also could not bolster Lilly's confidence, try as they might.

To everyone's surprise, there was one person who managed to offer Lilly a glimmer of optimism.

Wade McCord. Each weekend, he came to Bethany Springs, from Austin or San Antonio or wherever his legal work had him at the time. He spent Saturday afternoons quizzing Lilly on her essay writing and Algebra.

They set up a makeshift study in Amelia's kitchen. Every Saturday, from lunch to dinner, Lilly worked tirelessly. Wade left her with lessons to complete and books to read. Amelia always marveled at his patience and how well he explained difficult concepts. Whenever Lilly grew disheartened, he reminded her of how far she'd already come.

"You didn't know much about nursing care when you managed a gunshot wound. You've already done wonders. Imagine how far you'll go with a little schooling!"

Slowly, Lilly's confidence grew.

When it was time to travel to Galveston, Lilly claimed she was as ready as she'd ever be. Amelia announced they might as well all go and enjoy a few days at the shore. Wade invited himself along.

Naturally.

He never missed a chance to tag along.

The second morning in Galveston, Wade, Zach, and Daisy set off to escort Lilly to the school. They planned to explore the city while Lilly took her test. Amelia and Poppy stayed behind. Amelia noticed the youngest Muldoon often aggravated the middle one. She figured it would be best to keep them apart.

"You and I will walk the shore," she told Poppy after they left. "We'll make our own fun. And then I'll take you for a fancy lunch here in the hotel."

Poppy's eyes sparkled. "Just the two of us?"

"That's right." Amelia adjusted the girl's bonnet to shield her fair skin from the Texas sun.

"That sounds like fun, Miss Amelia. A lady's lunch. No boys allowed. I'll be the sergeant-at-arms."

Amelia rummaged through her bags, searching for her bonnet. "Of course. And for dessert you can have as much ice cream as you wish."

Poppy was rendered speechless. Her silence didn't last long. A moment later, she chattered excitedly, telling Mrs. Cavendish how she'd eat three whole scoops of ice cream.

The girl's excitement warmed Amelia's heart. When the Muldoon girls first came to the ranch, she'd noticed with wry amusement that the littlest Muldoon had a generous supply of sass. Anytime something troubled her, she'd fuss. Loudly. Usually at Daisy.

The trouble, from what Amelia gathered, started back when their uncle took them in. Since they'd just lost their parents, he'd overindulged them, especially the little girl. He'd likely chuckled at her mouthy replies and ignored her fiery temper. Little Poppy learned some mighty bad manners from her well-intentioned, soft-hearted uncle.

At first, Amelia said nothing, but then the little imp made a mistake. A big one.

On a Saturday not long after they'd arrived, Daisy had set a bowl of sugar down near the edge of the kitchen table, intending to pick it right back up. Poppy bounced into the kitchen and bumped the table, causing the porcelain bowl to shatter on the floor. Poppy fussed at Daisy, as if it were her fault. Amelia would have none of it.

"See that," Amelia said, pointing to the corner. *"It's a broom. This here's a dustpan. And here's a trash can. Clean up your mess. Come see me when you're done."*

Poppy spent the next hour sweeping, at first with tears threatening to fall from her eyes, but after an hour she was all smiles, and the broom had a name, Oscar, and Poppy had invited Oscar to have tea with her and Mrs. Cavendish.

Poppy had also apologized to Amelia, and to Daisy, and she promised to mend her ways. Since then, Amelia and Poppy had been fine friends. And fine friends have ice cream together, as often as they can.

Amelia and Poppy left the hotel, hand in hand headed down to the water.

Amelia glanced down the shoreline toward the nursing school. She couldn't see it from here, but she knew exactly where it was. She said a quick prayer and asked God to watch over sweet Lilly, to give the girl confidence and courage.

With a deep breath, she pushed her concerns aside. It was in God's hands now.

She and Poppy spent the morning enjoying the water and collecting seashells. The conversation turned to dogs and Poppy's dearest wish to have a puppy of her own. She told Amelia it was the thing she most wanted. Amelia promised to take her to visit ranchers in the area. If the girl wanted a pup, she'd do what she could to make that happen.

When it drew close to lunchtime they returned to the room and washed up for lunch. They both changed into clean dresses and went back downstairs. As they approached the dining room, Amelia saw someone who looked familiar. A jolt of surprise made her gasp softly.

"What is it, Miss Amelia?" Poppy asked.

"I don't believe it." Amelia ushered the girl to the side of the corridor. She ducked behind a large potted plant and drew Poppy near. Silently, she lifted a finger to her lips.

Poppy's eyes sparked with delight. She nodded and huddled closer to Amelia. They waited as a man and woman strolled out of the restaurant.

There in the hotel foyer stood Orville Childress, along with a female companion. Amelia might not have recognized Orville since he wasn't dressed in his usual formal attire. Orville looked like he'd spent the morning fishing. His companion, clad in a simple but sturdy frock, was dressed in the same casual garb. Her hair looked wind-blown, and her face pink from sun and wind.

Amelia noted the lady was pretty. Even more interesting was the sweet way Orville gazed at her. Yes, that was interesting indeed.

"Well, well," Amelia said softly.

"Did you enjoy your meal, Edith?" Orville asked.

"I certainly did, Orville. And you? Did you like your meal?" The woman laughed. "You'd better not say you like it better than my cooking."

"Nothing's as fine as your cooking, my little chickadee."

The woman wrapped her arms around Orville's arm and laughed again. "What a delightful vacation. I can't tell you how much this means to me."

"We'll do this as much as we like when I retire."

Orville and his companion wandered to the balcony windows and took in the view of the water.

The plant leaves blocked her view, so she parted them to better see Orville and his sweetheart. She tried to keep from chuckling. "I can't believe my eyes," she murmured. "I can't wait to tell Wade."

"Is that Santa Claus?" Poppy whispered.

Amelia smiled at the girl. With his portly frame, white hair and short beard, Orville looked a little like Santa. "No sweetheart. That's Governor Childress. He's an important man. He's also Virginia's father. You know? Simon's wife?"

Poppy nodded. "Yes ma'am. I recall."

After a moment, Poppy spoke again. "Why are we hiding?"

Amelia wasn't sure how to respond. She laughed sheepishly as she tried to summon a proper answer. Little Poppy had a good point.

She considered telling the girl, later, that she hid to spare Governor Childress any embarrassment. That wouldn't make much sense to a young girl, she realized. Maybe one day she'd explain and by then they could laugh at the memory.

Orville and his lady-friend wandered away from the window and down to the grand foyer. Dressed in his rumpled beach clothes, unshaven and wind-tousled, it was likely no one would recognize the governor. He'd be free to enjoy a pleasant afternoon with his sweetheart without too much trouble. And good for him, Amelia decided. She and Orville had a running rivalry, but she liked to think he might have found someone to care about.

Of course, she relished the sweet satisfaction of finding out his secret. She couldn't deny that. The notion made her smile inwardly.

"All right, Poppy. What do you say we go eat lunch?" Amelia held her hand out for the little girl to hold.

Soon they were sitting at a table beside a sunny window. They could see the whitecaps of the waves breaking on the sandy, Galveston beach. Amelia sat between Poppy and Mrs. Cavendish. Just the top of the doll's head was visible over the edge of the table, but Poppy still included Mrs. Cavendish in the conversation. Amelia found the girl's habit endearing and even addressed Mrs. Cavendish a time or two herself.

"I hope my sister's feeling all right," Poppy said as she took a bite of ice cream. "She says she feels seasick in the morning."

"Lilly?"

"No, ma'am. Daisy."

Amelia's breath stalled. She'd noticed Daisy looking a little wan at times and wondered if her sweet daughter-in-law might be in the family way. She didn't dare ask, however. She'd wait till Daisy and Zach wanted to share such news.

When Poppy finished her dessert, she excused herself from the table and took Mrs. Cavendish to the window.

Amelia remained seated at the table and relished the quiet moment. A rush of awe, happiness and wonder swirled inside her heart. Overcome, she folded her hands and let her gaze drift to the sailboats in the distance.

She noted all the fine things in her life.

Her three boys were all happily married to lovely girls. And God hadn't stopped there. The family had two new girls with Lilly and Poppy, and Elsie, the little orphan girl Daniel and Molly had taken in.

Her family meant everything to her, but she was grateful for other matters as well. After the terrible accident in Pineville, Daisy had healed completely. What was more, she might be expecting, just like Daniel's wife Molly and Simon's wife Virginia.

Then there was Lilly. God-willing, she would pass her exams and go off to nursing school.

Even Orville Childress was doing well for himself, it seemed. She smiled.

In addition to all that, Wade had helped her secure a contract to sell the sawmill. After Daisy's accident, she'd resolved to sell it and be done with the lumber trade.

Life was sweet. She felt a deep sense of gratitude as she gazed out the window and watched the tide roll to the beach. The waves rose, crested, and crashed on the shore with a slow rhythmic beauty.

Poppy glanced over her shoulder with a sweet, happy smile. Amelia gave the girl an answering smile. Yes, she did indeed feel blessed.

Amelia signaled the waiter for the bill. A few minutes later, he arrived, carrying a silver tray with a note. He set it down, bowed and hurried away.

She frowned. Inside, she found a message from Orville Childress, offering his best wishes and explaining he'd be honored to pay her lunch bill.

"That rascal," Amelia muttered with a chuckle. "That darn rascal."

He'd known she was there all along. And she'd played the fool, hiding behind a plant of all things. Orville would be laughing about this fine joke for years to come. To make matters worse, he'd tell the rest of the family when they came together for a meal or celebration. She sighed as she realized she'd never live it down.

Before she could give much more thought to Governor Childress, she noted Zach and Daisy's arrival. They crossed the dining room, smiling broadly. Wade and Lilly followed. Lilly wore a grin while Wade looked a little flustered but happy. The poor fellow had likely been as nervous as Lilly and relieved it was all over. Thank goodness.

Poppy rushed to meet the group, hugging Lilly first and next Daisy. The family gathered around the table, each of them talking and laughing about the events of the morning. Lilly made high marks on her exams and passed easily.

Lilly was pleased and perhaps a little surprised it was all over.

Wade slumped in his chair, looking worn out. He told Amelia and the rest of the group he'd been more nervous than he could recall. "Thinking about that danged nursing test was worse than all the times I've argued a case before the high courts."

Daisy thanked him for all his help and spoke of Lilly's talent for caregiving.

"She's a wonder," Daisy said. "I'm amazed by my sister's passion. And grateful too. Especially for what she did for Zach."

Amelia nodded. Thank heavens for Lilly's skill. If she hadn't tended to Zach... well, Amelia didn't like to think about that sort of thing. It was just the type of worry that woke her in the dark of night.

Zach spoke last. He'd never had a doubt that Lilly would do fine on her tests. He'd always known. She'd cared for him, tending to him where there was no other medical help. She'd be a fine nurse one day soon.

"Lilly's going to be a blessing to those in need," he said quietly. "I've known all along."

Lilly teared up, too overcome to reply.

Amelia smiled, her eyes stinging with happy tears. Lilly was on her way. She'd start classes the beginning of September. Amelia's boys were safe and happy as were their families. Life was good. More than good. With a grateful heart she gave thanks for all her blessings.

The End

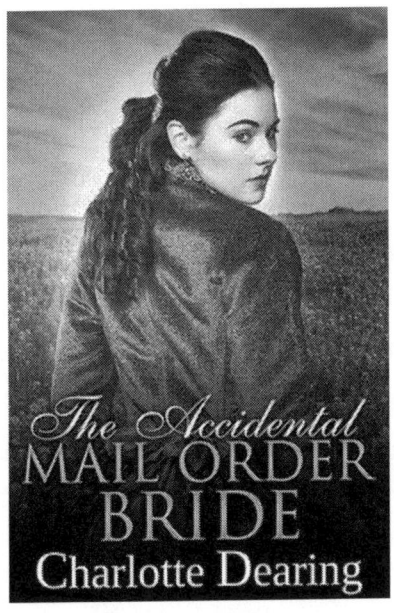

Ezra McCord feels that God has entrusted him with a small boy to care for, and he's determined to do whatever it takes to raise the child right. Even if it means taking a wife. Having someone to clean and cook and take care of Harvey would be fine by him. That's all Isabelle wants as well, but things take an unexpected turn.

Books by Charlotte Dearing

Mail Order Providence
Mail Order Sarah
Mail Order Ruth

<u>Brides of Bethany Springs Series</u>
To Charm a Scarred Cowboy
Kiss of the Texas Maverick
Vow of the Texas Cowboy
The Accidental Mail Order Bride
Starry-Eyed Mail Order Bride
An Inconvenient Mail Order Bride
Amelia's Storm

<u>The Bluebonnet Brides Collection</u>
Mail Order Grace
Mail Order Rescue
Mail Order Faith
Mail Order Hope
Mail Order Destiny
Love's Destiny

Sign up at <u>www.charlottedearing.com</u> to be notified of special offers and announcements.

Manufactured by Amazon.ca
Bolton, ON